"The year I stopped trying."

Also by Katie Heaney

Girl Crushed

Never Have I Ever: My Life (So Far) Without a Date

Dear Emma

Public Relations

*Would You Rather? A Memoir of Growing Up
and Coming Out*

"The year I stopped trying."

—a novel,
by Katie
Heaney

Alfred A. Knopf
New York

THIS IS A BORZOI BOOK PUBLISHED BY ALFRED A. KNOPF

This is a work of fiction. Names, characters, places, and incidents either are the product of the author's imagination or are used fictitiously. Any resemblance to actual persons, living or dead, events, or locales is entirely coincidental.

Text copyright © 2021 by Katie Heaney
Jacket design by Casey Moses

All rights reserved. Published in the United States by Alfred A. Knopf, an imprint of Random House Children's Books, a division of Penguin Random House LLC, New York.

Knopf, Borzoi Books, and the colophon are registered trademarks of Penguin Random House LLC.

Visit us on the Web! GetUnderlined.com

Educators and librarians, for a variety of teaching tools, visit us at RHTeachersLibrarians.com

Library of Congress Cataloging-in-Publication Data is available upon request.
ISBN 978-0-593-11828-3 (trade) — ISBN 978-0-593-11830-6 (ebook)

The text of this book is set in 11.2-point Gamma ITC Std.
Interior design by Cathy Bobak

Printed in the United States of America
November 2021
10 9 8 7 6 5 4 3 2 1
First Edition

For my brothers, Joe and Dan

The first time was a mistake.

I don't like to admit that, because I think this whole thing would be cooler if I'd meant to do it from the beginning for some good reason, or even *a* reason. But the truth is that one day, after ten years without incident, I just forgot.

There wasn't anything unusual going on that week. I worked my usual shift at La Baguette, got home, did what was left of my homework, watched a little TV, and went to sleep. The next morning I got up, ate the same breakfast, made the same peanut butter and jelly sandwich and put the same chips and carrots in little plastic bags, and drove my brother, Peter, and me the same way to school. I walked into first period three minutes before the bell, completely prepared for another normal day. Then class started, and the teacher asked us to hand in our homework . . . and my stomach fell into my feet. My face burned. I felt faint and dizzy and a little like I might throw up. Because I had not done my AP U.S. history homework. Somehow, in the list of things I had to do the night before, this one had gotten lost. As everyone around me dug through their bags for their short essays on Manifest Destiny, I flipped through my planner and scanned yesterday's to-do items. And there it was, with a line drawn through it, like everything else on the page. But I had not written that essay. I looked through my folder, just in case, but I knew there was nothing to find.

I sat there, sweating, for the rest of class, planning what I'd say to Mr. Delaney to let him know I knew I'd made a mistake and I'd never do it again if somehow he could find it in him to forgive me. I could offer to do a makeup assignment, a five- or ten-page paper on a topic of his choosing. Or I could pretend I *had* done the homework but had packed my bag wrong because of unspecified stressors at home. I could say I'd gotten home late from work and set a 4:00 a.m. alarm to finish, but then my phone died, and I was almost late for school. He might believe me and offer me half credit to bring it in tomorrow. I weighed whether the damage to my dignity would be worth it if he did.

Maybe I would just run.

Class ended. I hovered for a few moments over my desk, slowly gathering my belongings, waiting for Mr. Delaney to call me over to explain myself. He had his shirtsleeves rolled up just slightly, revealing powerful-looking wrists and the merest glimpse of a tattoo faded navy. He was a former marine, and the rumor was that under his shirt and slacks he was covered from neck to ankle in tattoos. He loved pop quizzes and had a particular knack for calling on people exactly when they'd decided it was safe to zone out. Once, allegedly, he'd even offered an open-book final, only to retract the open-book part on the day of the exam. Mr. Delaney was not a teacher who could be counted on for grace.

Finally he looked up and saw me there, watching him as the next class's students started filtering into the classroom. "Yes, Mary?" he said. "Did you have a question?"

"No," I said automatically. "Sorry."

"See you tomorrow," he said firmly, and a little patronizingly. So I turned, and I walked out.

And that was it. After fifty-two minutes of agony and anxiety, my heart rate up and my head woozy and hot, it was over? I wasn't relieved; I was furious. I consoled myself by thinking he'd hold me after class the next day, after he'd had a chance to go through the essays, but he never handed them back. He just talked about the themes he'd seen, our collective mistakes. At the beginning of class, my shoulders were tensed up near my ears, but the more time passed, the lower they fell, until it felt safe to confirm: I'd gotten away with it. I had failed to turn in homework to the scariest teacher at school, and he didn't even notice. So what had all that worrying and all that guilt been for?

The next time I didn't do something, it would be on purpose.

Mr. Bartlett, my AP calculus teacher, offers weekly extra credit so everyone doesn't fail. He assigns the homework, then gives an optional extra page we can do for ten points. You don't even have to get the answers right—you just have to show you honestly tried, and ten points are yours. For a long time I resented this system, because you could essentially fail the homework and get, like, twenty-seven out of fifty, and if you even half-assed the extra credit, you wound up with a thirty-seven, which is a C.

I rarely needed the extra credit to clear an A, but I did it every week, to get a higher one. With extra credit I'd get fifty-five or sixty out of fifty on my homework, which left me with a running total of something like 110 percent. Which is still just an A, and not even the highest A in the class: Ellen Barnes has 132 percent, because she also gets perfect scores on all the tests, whereas I usually score in the low nineties or, on a bad day, the high eighties. But I figured that if I somehow bombed the final, I'd thank my earlier self for banking all those points. But it didn't seem all that likely that I'd suddenly fail.

So one week, when Mr. Bartlett offers my class page forty-two of the workbook for extra credit, I just . . . don't do it. I hand in my assigned pages, and when I get them back the next day (forty-seven out of fifty), Mr. Bartlett has written a little note at the top: *No extra credit this week?* Next to this he's drawn a little smiley face, and if I had to pinpoint a trigger that set this whole thing off, I'd choose that stupid, smug, patronizing little smiley face. That smiley face thought it had me all figured out. *Oh, yeah?* I thought. *Watch me.*

The next time Mr. Bartlett offers extra credit, I don't do it. Again. This time no smiley face. This time he asks to see me after class.

"I noticed you didn't do the extra credit again, and I just wanted to make sure everything's okay," he says. His brow is furrowed, and he clasps his hands together in concern. He has the hairiest knuckles I have ever seen. I don't want to be caught staring, but my eyes are drawn back again and again. Little hairs poke out from under his wedding band, and for some reason it's this part that disgusts me most.

"It's not required, right?" I ask.

"Well, no."

"Then I don't need to do it," I say.

The look on Mr. Bartlett's face sends shame radiating down my body. Even my ankles blush. But I stand my ground, and then he shrugs. "Okay," he says. And I leave.

———

I go home that day expecting an interrogation. I think my transgression should be visible on my face: this is not a girl who bothers with extra credit. But nobody says anything. I linger in the kitchen after setting the table while my mom cooks two dinners: one for herself and one for my dad, my brother, and me. My mom's latest diet dictates that she not eat anything with seeds, which pretty much just leaves cauliflower, as far as I can tell. I would have thought there were only two, maybe three, ways to eat cauliflower, but my mom has carried on this way for weeks.

"What's for dinner?" I ask.

"Beef Stroganoff," she says.

"I meant for you."

"Just a simple stir-fry," she says. Her forehead looks sweaty.

"Is that real rice, or—"

"Cauliflower."

I nod. Linger.

"How was school?" she asks, suspicious.

"Fine," I say. "I got in trouble for not doing extra credit for calculus."

"You got in trouble?" She doesn't even stop stirring.

"Well, my teacher asked me about it."

"But you still have an A," she says.

"Yeah." I shift from one foot to the other, refolding a napkin that doesn't need it.

"That doesn't sound like trouble."

"Yeah, I guess not," I say. My stomach sinks. She's right.

———

It isn't about attention.

Getting good grades, being on time, raising my hand, finishing every available vocabulary book so my teacher has to place a special order just for me—*that* gets me attention. Or it used to. In middle school, maybe, I was the best and most favored, but I'm not anymore. My practice ACT scores max out at thirty. I'm not ranked in my year's top-ten students. The last I checked, I was number twenty-one. Out of 423, sure. But still. My GPA is 3.94, largely because no amount of studying can make me understand the practical purpose of math beyond the algebra level, and this attitude shows up in the perfunctory nature of my homework (or so I've been told). I'm worse at physics, but at least physics makes intuitive sense: things go up and come back down. I've seen this happen.

The problem, as I'm coming to understand it, is that I'm very familiar with what happens after I do what I'm supposed to do. It used to be that when a teacher I liked handed back a paper I got a perfect score on, with a little note about what a pleasure it was to read, I'd get a little glowing ball of pride in my belly. And then I'd start the next paper, or start studying for the next test. I'd do the work. I'd get the gentle praise. Over and over, year after year. The tests and the worksheets and the essays run together. The pride is replaced by a dull relief. Somewhere along the way, I realize, my motivation shifted from chasing the medium-good feeling I got from every A to avoiding whatever I might feel if I got anything less. The result is the same either way, so everyone else with a stake in my performance is happy. But I'm not happy. If I keep doing the same thing while expecting a different result, I'm the crazy one.

When I decide to stop trying, I begin to see my manager at my part-time job at La Baguette differently. La Baguette is what is known as a "fast-casual" establishment, which means that there isn't a drive-through, but there isn't really any cooking being done, either. Our soups arrive frozen, in barrels. Our bread and pastries are delivered by truck. We offer the impression of a healthy lunch: half a sandwich, half a salad. Our combination meal is called a "half 'n' half." On the menu behind the counter, on all the signs in our windows, this term is pluralized as "half 'n' halfs," which I hate, though Jerry has repeatedly and defensively told me it is grammatically correct.

Jerry is my manager, a guy who wears his dark gray hair slicked straight back. It's easy to imagine him in "the club" in a fake silk shirt, sending drinks to women half his age. But at work he wears polo shirts, tucked into khakis. We all wear polos: it's La Baguette law. Any color is fine. I get mine in taupe and peach and sickly green—whatever is cheapest at Kohl's. Over the past year and a half I've worked with girls who come in on their first day wearing Lacoste or some other eighty-dollar polo, but you can't multipurpose a work polo, and anyone employed there more than a day learns as much. The smell of a La Baguette polo is instantaneous, unmistakable, nonremovable. The restaurant itself smells fine, but the way the aromas of warm bread and Caesar dressing and clam chowder mix in the air and settle into the cotton is just—well, it's unforgettable. I once told my work friend Kristy they should bottle the smell and sell it, but she didn't laugh, because she doesn't have a sense of humor. That's probably the main thing holding back our friendship.

Today when I clock in at work, Jerry tells me I'm on dishwasher duty, which says something about my abilities as a cash-register operator, and probably my looks, whether he admits it or not. Kristy, for instance, is never put on dishwasher duty. She is smiley and pretty and wears a lot of eyeliner and looks at least three years older than me, though, in fact, I am older by five months. When I asked her when her birthday was, she got nervous and weird, like she thought I was going to buy her a present or something. I may call her my "friend," but I am neither delusional nor rich. We don't go to the same school, and we will never, ever see each other outside of La Baguette. When one of us quits, we will never see each other again, and we won't miss each other. But for now, in the context of this faux-French café, she is the best I have.

And here I thought I'd been extra friendly to the customers lately.

Dishwashing at La Baguette is a male-coded job, because the other girls find it gross to touch other people's partly eaten food, which it is, but that aside, I don't really mind it. I don't have to talk to anyone, and the work runs in an endless, predictable cycle: I collect the bins of dirty dishes, scrape the leftover food bits into the garbage, load the dirty dishes into the plastic racks, slide the plastic racks into the industrial washer, and pull the handle that closes the doors. The water whooshes, and while I wait, I rinse off the trays and stack them to dry. When the dishes are clean (and hot), I load them on a rolling cart and roll my way to behind the counter, where I unload them: the full plates, then the crescent-shaped half plates, the bowls, the mugs. Same thing with the utensils. Sometimes we run low on a particular item—usually the half plates—and I make it my mission to hover around the dining room, looking for whoever is taking so goddamn long to finish their Asian chicken salad. Making eye contact once reminds them that this is called a *fast*-casual establishment for a reason, but any more than that and I risk them complaining about customer service on Yelp. When someone complains about customer service on Yelp, Jerry sends a scolding email to everyone who was working that day, and those emails take me a good three days to get over. Of course, going forward, I plan not to internalize them at all.

But just in case.

It's slow, so I run a partially loaded rack through the washer. Jerry happens to walk through the back of the restaurant just then, and when he sees it, he tells me I shouldn't run the dishwasher for a half-empty rack, because it's a waste of water.

"I see it more as half-full," I say.

He does not laugh.

So now we know Jerry is in a mood.

(Also, the thing is, if I *don't* run the dishwasher for a half-empty rack, then I'm doing nothing. And I get in trouble for doing nothing. Jerry would argue that there's never any reason to be doing nothing, but you can sweep the carpeted dining room only so many times while the restaurant is still open. The soap dispenser can only be so full; the door, only so handprint-free.)

Later I'm in the dining room, sweeping the carpet. The broom's red bristles are bent out of shape and twisted at one end, so the trick is to sweep using the other end, in short, quick strokes in the direction of the dustpan. There is a vacuum, but we're not allowed to use it while the restaurant is open, but we're also not allowed to wait until closing time to deal with the floor. My sweeping movements are jerky and strange, and I can feel sweat start to pool in the small of my back.

It remains surprising to me that nobody can tell that I am different now. I haven't done extra credit in two weeks, I've even been lightly scolded for it, and as far as anyone at La Baguette knows, I have carried on just the same as always. I don't talk about my grades, and no one I work with goes to the same school, but I get the feeling they just know what kind of student I am, and by extension, what kind of person. Which is to say: uncool.

I am going to have to step it up.

———

On Friday I have a physics test. I have an A in physics, but unlike my other A's, it is somewhat hard-won. Questions about two trains speeding toward each other and when will they collide—I hate that. I understand why these questions should matter to someone, but I can't seem to make them matter to me. Instead, I wonder: *Shouldn't there be some sort of system in place to avoid collisions like these? Who green-lit both trains to run on the same track?* Then I think of the few times I've been on a train, and another train going the opposite direction shot past mine. Then I'd wonder, again, why they'd set the tracks so close to each other. They shouldn't have to be that close.

So physics homework is the most time-consuming homework I have, and the tests are the hardest. I usually start three nights ahead and make a study guide, and then study my study guide between classes for the next two days, in addition to reviewing my notes at night. When I succeed, it's because of sheer memorization. That didn't used to bother me. My classmates are always loudly complaining about the pointlessness of anything we learn, and I'm always, like, *Shut upppp.* That's just what school is. You're not original for hating homework.

But now I am one of them. So what I do is I deliberately don't study.

The test is about vectors and scalars. On Tuesday Mr. Fullerton draws an x-axis and a y-axis on the board, and then a triangle, where the x-axis is one of its sides. He labels the diagonal line A, and the vertical line $Ay = A \sin\Theta$, and the side along the x-axis, $Ax = A \cos\Theta$. I stare at it for so long it starts to seem funny. *What does it mean?* I think, laughing silently to myself. I'm shaking, and my eyes well up with tears. It's the funniest thing I've ever seen in my life, this triangle. *What does it mean???* My tablemate, Zac Notopoulos, slides as far across his chair from me as it is possible to be without falling off. Which is pretty rich considering how often he cheats off me. That day, for the first time, he doesn't, and I feel victorious. Someone has noticed.

I got a B+ on the physics test. To be more precise: eighty-nine percent. I'm so mad I almost throw it on the floor, but it's just two pieces of paper stapled together, and it wouldn't be satisfying enough to be worth having to pick it back up.

All that not-studying! You'd think I could have at least managed a C.

It annoys me to know I'm absorbing material I don't need and don't want without my consent. Just by being here, in this classroom, for fifty-two minutes a day, I am learning something, whether I want to or not.

At lunch I sink into my seat, defeated. I have made myself a turkey-and-Swiss sandwich plus a bag of baby carrots and a bag of two Oreos. My friend Cara sits down soon after me with her tray. It's Tuesday: breadsticks day. A paper cup with four fat beige breadsticks wilts alongside a smaller paper cup full of microwaved tomato sauce. The sauce used to come in plastic cups, but the school Sierra Club successfully petitioned to change it. So now at the end of every day the garbage cans in the cafeteria are full of food and paper instead of food and plastic.

Cara hands me a breadstick, and I give her half of my sandwich. I dunk the breadstick in the sauce and take a big, doughy bite. It tastes like nothing. I love it.

"I got a B plus," I say, muffled by breadstick. "In physics."

"I got a C," says Cara. She's in the physics class right after mine. Across the span of our friendship, we have shared only two classes: freshman English, which is where we met, and sophomore biology, where we dissected a fetal pig. Cara did all the cutting, because I was afraid that if I touched the pig with my knife it would scream, and then I'd have to kill myself. That first day, seeing the pigs all stacked up in a big plastic bag, Mrs. Pullman plunking them down on desks one by one—it was horrible. I remember thinking: *Is this really necessary?* I avoid the science hallway every November (pig slaughter season), but I can still smell it.

I was annoyed by Cara's nonchalance in the literal face of a dead pig, and I'm annoyed by it now. *Must be nice to have so many C's they no longer mean anything to you,* I think.

Our diverging work ethics are one of several reasons we are no longer as close as we once were. Another is that Cara has gotten approximately ten times hotter since freshman year, while I look exactly the same. When we met, we looked like peers: our matching braces; my flat medium-brown hair and her frizzy black pouf, which she spent hours frying with a straightener each morning; my scrawny legs in too-short jeans and the chest she flattened with sports bras and covered in oversize flannel shirts. We both lost the braces, but she's freed the boobs and mastered something called the "curly girl method." I should have seen it coming in our names alone: "Cara Shah" sounds like a model. "Mary Davies" sounds like a librarian.

"How did you do that?" I ask.

"Do what?"

"Get a C."

She looks at me like I'm the stupidest girl alive. But I'm not. I got a B+ on a physics test without studying.

"I don't understand the question," she says.

"Never mind," I say. I don't really feel like explaining myself or telling her about my self-deterioration project. She would think I'm insane, or worse, trying to be more like her. I am still disappointed when she shrugs and changes the subject to Theo, the boy she likes, who is two years older, in college two states over, and has led her on for as long as I've known her.

But then she gives me an idea. Maybe *that's* what I need: someone to distract me, and drag me down with him. Maybe I need to get a boyfriend.

———

That night I google "how to get a boyfriend" and read everything I can find.

I watch a YouTube video by a guy named Josh, who is probably my age. More than a million people have watched this video. He's wearing a baseball cap backward over blondish-brown hair. He has blue eyes and a little bit of acne—just enough, not so much that it's a medical issue. He is, objectively, cute. He has blindingly white teeth, though I know there's a filter for that. Josh is the type of boy that Cara would pick out for me: not old or dangerous enough for her but still well out of my reach. She thinks I think everyone is out of my reach, which is not true. Just the good-looking boys.

Josh's first tip is "get his attention."

Brilliant, I think. *How?* I think.

Josh does not specify. He moves quickly on to number two: "confidence."

I close out of the video. *Thanks for nothing, Josh.*

Other advice I read includes wearing my hair in a ponytail, smiling a lot, wearing skirts, and teasing them. I go to my closet and dig out a pleated skirt I bought freshman year as part of a *Gossip Girl* costume that made me look like a private school student who got lost. There are "C" and "B" patches (for Constance Billard School for Girls) still stitched to the bottom right side, so I root around in the kitchen junk drawer looking for the seam ripper.

"What are you looking for?" my mom asks. She is reading a diet book, highlighter in hand, at the table. She hates when I rummage.

"Seam ripper," I say.

"What for?"

"Ripping a seam?" I say.

My mom *tsks*, annoyed. "Yeah, on what?"

"Just an old skirt," I say. "I'm not ruining anything."

"Okay . . . ," she says, skeptically. As if I'm planning to take the seam ripper into her room and tear up the bedspread or something.

I return to my room with the seam ripper and start dissecting my skirt. The patches are handmade from felt and easy to remove, but they leave behind a number of loose black threads. I clip them as neatly to the skirt as possible, but if you got close enough, you could tell something used to be there. Somehow I don't think this will be an issue.

I keep the patch as a memento of a rare battle between Cara and me that I won: I got to be Serena; she had to be Blair. She says that's what she always wanted, but it's not. Anyone who's actually read the books and says they want to be anyone other than Serena is lying or stupid. And Cara isn't stupid.

The next day I'm wearing my ex-*Gossip Girl* skirt and a white T-shirt and my hair in the highest ponytail I can muster. When I see Cara at lunch, she's, like, "Is that your Catholic school skirt?"

Back in freshman year, Cara didn't wear her costume to school on Halloween the way we'd planned—an implicit acknowledgment, I thought, of Blair's inferiority. It is at least fifty percent her fault that nobody knew who I was supposed to be.

"Gossip Girl," I correct.

"Why are you wearing that?" she asks.

I consider not telling her. I know that if I tell Cara I'm looking for a boyfriend, she'll lose her mind and try way too hard to help. I know this because not long after we met, I offhandedly mentioned wanting a boyfriend, and she took it as a personal challenge. She checked out half a dozen relationship and self-help books from the library, and came over after school to read the best parts aloud. She wrote mantras on my bathroom mirror in lipstick (which my mom then made me scrub off), and insisted we start wearing perfume, even though it gave me a headache. She wrote a list of our grade's eligible bachelors on a piece of notebook paper and compiled three likes and dislikes for each boy, based entirely on their social media. I loved this about her—how sincerely she believed she could get boyfriends for us both if only we wanted it badly enough—but she kept it going for months after I'd given up and wanted to talk about something else, anything else.

I give in anyway. I tell her about my research. When she's done laughing at me, she suggests we draw up a list of candidates.

The top contender, as always, is Brandon Durchek. Brandon is second-tier popular, reluctantly accepted by the first tier, though frequently reminded of his place via ritualized teasing. His family has money but not *that* much money; he's athletic but not a star; he's generically attractive but too pudgy to be hot outright. Cara likes to call him an investment boyfriend, which means he will appreciate in value over time.

"He's gonna be hot in three years," she says. "Trust me."

This, to me, seems like a long time to wait.

For some reason Brandon does seem to have a sort of crush on me. I am oblivious to most forms of flirting (not that I'm the target very often), but with him it would be hard not to catch on. Once in earth science he asked to borrow my ChapStick, and I was so stunned that I just handed it over. He rubbed the balm over his lips, and when he handed it back, he said,

"Now it's like we kissed." He says things like that to a lot of girls, though.

Brandon has conspicuously never had a girlfriend, and I think it's mostly desperation that propels him toward me. It's this same quality that desexualizes him completely.

Besides, we have no mutual friends, no shared interest, nothing bringing us together. Short of me sticking a note in his locker, how would I—as Josh advised—get his attention? And do I even want it?

With these arguments I'm able to convince Cara to move on.

Behind door number two is Andre Cappelli, my sometime project partner when assigned by last name. We are the kind of acquaintances who give each other quick affirming nods when we see each other in the hallways or the cafeteria, as if to say, "It's nice to know you're still here." Andre is cute, but three inches shorter than me, at least, and I am not that tall for a girl. He also wears the same Pink Floyd T-shirt three days a week, and I'm pretty sure he doesn't even listen to Pink Floyd. If Brandon constitutes a social step up, Andrew is a lateral move.

He also gets really good grades, and that is *not* the point.

"What about Mitch?" I say.

Cara's jaw hits the floor.

Mitch Kulikosky was, technically, my boyfriend for three days in sixth grade, back when he was a dork with greasy hair who drew anime in class. I once let slip that I liked him to my then best friend and current enemy Hanna Hughes. She asked him out on my behalf; he said yes; and for three days I said nothing, just to see what having a boyfriend did to change my life. Mitch and I didn't talk in person once, only texting each other a few times to say precisely nothing. By Friday of that week I was bored, so I dumped him via messenger Hanna.

Let me amend that. "Enemy" is too strong a word. I don't wish her ill or anything. What's a good term for someone whose existence no longer matters to you because they've made it clear that yours no longer matters to them?

In the years since, Mitch traded anime for weed, dyed his hair pink, and got insanely, stupidly hot. Nobody saw it coming, least of all me. He was constantly in trouble and never at school. I saw him maybe once a month, always in the parking lot, often headed out when everyone else was headed in, or vice versa.

"Are you serious?" says Cara, and I can tell she's a little impressed.

"He's so hot," I say. "And we do have a history."

We both laugh. Today is a day I feel lucky to have her.

Cara tells me she thinks I should focus on someone more practical, but I decide to put all my boyfriend-getting eggs in Mitch's basket. She says, "He's like a shadow. I don't remember the last time I even saw him."

This, I think, is one of his best qualities.

Anyway, all I really need is the reputation by association. Last time we went out he was a nerd and only made me seem nerdier for being willing to date him. He owes me. If people hear we're going out, they'll think differently of me, and maybe that's what I need in order to think differently of myself.

As it stands, my self-deterioration project is in need of a boost. After the eighty-nine in physics, my reflexes took over, and I turned in what I know was a perfect English lit paper. Perfect five-paragraph structure, perfect grammar, perfectly half-interesting thesis, the whole thing. Sometimes English papers are so easy I feel like I'm cheating, when really all I'm doing is exactly what my teacher told me to do.

————

Thinking about Mitch provides a welcome distraction from thinking about council, which I have after school once a week. So far this year I've looked forward to meeting day, because meeting day means I don't have to go to work and I don't have to drive Peter home—he takes the bus, and I get the car to myself, taking the long way home, listening to music as loud as I want. But today is different, because today a writer for *The Argus*, our student newspaper, is attending the meeting to report on the council's fall semester initiatives. This is a problem for me, because that writer happens to be Hanna Hughes.

Until last month, at one earlier such meeting, Hanna and I hadn't spoken in more than two years. It didn't feel good when we stopped talking, but over time I'd grown used to it, and I assumed she had, too. We didn't even speak directly to each other at the meeting, but speaking around each other, in each other's general direction, made continuing our mutual ignoring impossible. It started seeming . . . rude. So lately, when we pass in the hallway, we exchange nods or sometimes half waves, hands momentarily released from the grip around our respective backpack straps. Each time I walk by her, I'm convinced that nobody in the history of humanity has ever nodded or waved more weirdly than me. Each time we acknowledge each other, I'm forced to remember how easy being around her used to be.

Hanna is already seated when I walk in. With her reporter's notebook and pen in hand, she looks so much the part of a real, serious reporter it's hard not to smile. Her hair is newly braided and wrapped into a high bun, and I don't recognize the gold wire-rimmed grandpa-style glasses. Her eyesight's been terrible since before I met her, but after an awkward patch with too-small pink metal frames in seventh grade, she's managed to make cool glasses her signature. I think about telling her I like them but convince myself to stay strong. She is no longer interested in my friendship, and I don't want to embarrass myself by acting like I still want hers.

Student council meets in a sort of half room separated from Mr. Berg's honors freshman English class by a row of filing cabinets and a fold-up conference table where we keep our mailbox and our snacks. Ingrid, the president, is here, too—thank God—and writes our agenda on the whiteboard from her kneeled perch on the sagging maroon couch below it. I grab one of the brownies Ingrid's arranged on a plate and take a seat opposite Hanna, who smiles at me with a closed mouth.

Soon Missy, the vice president (no brownie), and Philip, the treasurer (two brownies), arrive and take their places on either side of Ingrid's thick purple council binder. Ingrid greets them both too cheerily, apparently for Hanna's benefit, and caps her marker (also purple) triumphantly.

"Okay!" she says. "Let's do a quick roll call, and then we can get started."

There are exactly four of us, each of whom she just identified, but Ingrid loves a formality. As the junior class council, we serve a largely symbolic function, meant mostly as a rehearsal for those who will go on to serve in the senior class council. Below us are the freshman and sophomore class representatives (five per year), who are largely powerless but who are occasionally invited to vote on matters like Homecoming theme and whether to raise funds via bake sale or coupon-book raffle. Ingrid and I were both elected class representatives as freshmen and are the only ones still serving. Did I think Ingrid would offer me the VP slot in recognition of my years of service? Yes. Was I surprised when she instead offered it to Missy Chambers, in order to secure the vocal Young Life voting bloc? No, I was not. Secretary suited me just fine. Too well, probably.

We each recite our names, and then Ingrid makes a big show of welcoming Hanna. "Journalism is so important," she says defensively.

Hanna shares another tight smile. "Just pretend I'm not here," she says, glancing quickly at Ingrid and then, unnervingly, at me. "I mean, until I have questions."

"Okay!" says Ingrid, consulting the agenda on the whiteboard. "Let's check the suggestion box?" She gives me a pointed look, and I understand I'm meant to pretend this is something we do every meeting. I get up and remove the shoebox that hangs from the council door on a string and am surprised—and then not—to find there's actually something in it. I unfold the piece of paper and read it aloud: "Host a self-defense workshop for girls." This suggestion is written in purple pen in what appears to be deliberately bad handwriting. Philip and I exchange a look, and I shove the paper into my pocket.

"That's an interesting idea!" Ingrid says. "We could check with local martial arts schools to see if anyone would volunteer to teach a couple classes after school?"

"Nobody's going to stay after school for that," says Missy.

Hanna starts to write something in her notebook, and we all freeze, watching her.

"Obviously, there are people interested, if it was in the box," says Ingrid with a falsely cheery optimism we all recognize as a threat.

"One person," clarifies Philip.

"I think it sounds cool," I say. I can't help it; I feel bad. "But I think it should be open to all gender identities."

Hanna pulls her notebook closer and scrawls something in it.

"Smart," says Ingrid, smiling through gritted teeth. If Hanna weren't here, there's no way she'd let me win that easily. Though if Hanna weren't here, we probably wouldn't be discussing this idea at all. There may be a point about government accountability to be made here, but Ingrid interrupts my thought to suggest we move on.

The rest of the meeting is dedicated to choosing a teacher and a student of the month (junior council chooses a junior but also chooses among three freshmen and sophomores nominated by their respective class officers) and brainstorming daily activities for "Make a Difference Week." School policy dictates that any council-led volunteering or fundraising be apolitical (as if that's a thing), which makes this process fairly predictable: there will be toy drives and food banks and nursing-home visits and picking up trash on the side of the road. Ingrid may want to believe her ideas are radical, but anything we get approved will always be something somebody's done before. When she and I were freshman reps, a senior tried to set up a pen-pal program between students and incarcerated people, and the PTA just about burned down the school.

We wrap up a few minutes early, and Ingrid reluctantly asks Hanna if she has any questions.

Hanna trails her pen down the notepad as she rereads her notes. "I don't think so," she says. "Maybe just—do you have a timeline for the self-defense thing?"

Ingrid smiles. "TBD."

Hanna returns the smile. "I'll follow up," she says. "I think it's a cool idea."

Ingrid seems anxious, though I don't think she needs to be. Nothing we talked about was remotely controversial, or even interesting. Missy yawns loudly and taps away at her phone. Philip is packaging two additional brownies in a ziplock bag he pulled from his backpack. I feel equal parts protective of and depressed by this room, this miniature make-believe government I'm part of. I wonder what Hanna thinks of the person I've become without her friendship, though maybe she doesn't think of me at all. When she waves goodbye and walks out, I wait a full five minutes just to make sure I don't see her in the parking lot. I hope she doesn't come to another meeting for a very long time.

———

At the dinner table my brother is in trouble for not turning something in, and I think, *That's* my *thing*. Only it isn't really, because I haven't gotten caught yet, and he does it all the time.

Today it was Spanish homework, which to me makes it all the more ridiculous, because Spanish is so easy. *El sacapuntas*: pencil sharpener. My favorite word. I have taken high school Spanish for four years (I started early, in eighth grade) and I still sound like a robot when I speak it, but nobody seems to care much. None of our white Spanish teachers even try to put on an accent. Then again, I find it annoying when a classmate leans *too* hard into it, rolling every *r* two beats too long. I'm thinking of you, Stephanie Carroll.

My mom is frowning at Peter over her cauliflower pizza, and my dad is giving him a lecture about responsibility. Then my mom tells him to clean his room tonight—that's part of the punishment—and again I wonder why it is that my brother was given the bigger bedroom, and the one marginally farther down the hall from my parents. Sometimes they threaten to make us switch, but they'll never do it. It would involve too much work for them. And I don't want the bigger bedroom as a castoff. I want it to have been mine all along. But the room that's now mine was painted pink when we moved in, marking it *Girl's Room*, so here we are.

"Didn't you put it in the planner we got you?" my mom is saying.

Peter shrugs. "Yeah."

"What are you going to do when we aren't here to hold your hand?" says my dad.

"Where are you going . . . ?" says Peter. He's making fun of them, but they don't seem to notice. I'm jealous of his nerve, and I hate him for it at the same time.

"Not us—you. When *you* go to college," says my dad.

"Ohhhh," says Peter.

I used to enjoy these interrogations. I didn't feel good about it, but I felt a righteous pleasure watching my little brother cower and stare at his plate. It felt good to watch justice unfold: the scolding, the pleading, the punishment. It meant there was a reason I did what I did the way I did it. It meant he was on the wrong path and I was on the right one. Now I wonder: *What's at the end of it, anyway? What if all this effort turns out not to matter at all? Who'd be humiliated then?*

My parents are so proud of me. I've never questioned that, and I know that makes me lucky. But if I stopped doing what they tell me to do—if I stayed out past midnight and I stopped doing homework and my GPA dropped and I announced I didn't want to go to college after all—what would happen? I have no idea. I don't know what our relationship outside my achievements and my obedience looks like. I don't know who I am without grades and rules. What if there isn't anything else?

———

The first time I don't turn in an assignment on purpose, I choose Spanish. I think of it as an homage to Peter. Also, Señora Nelson is the teacher who scares me least. I'm casting a wide net with my refusal to comply, trying not to overwhelm any single teacher at once. (Later I will recognize this as another amateurish failure to fail, because I am ultimately still putting my teachers' feelings before my own goals. But it is still early, and I am still learning.)

I can't believe how easy it is. Señora Nelson tells us to pass our papers to the front. I take the papers from the girl behind me, and then I hand them forward, without adding anything of my own to the stack. She won't even know my homework is missing until after class, or maybe even after school—whenever she does her grading. My face feels hot, but I survive it once again. Nobody yells at me or throws me into the street. Nothing happens at all.

We begin the day's lesson: the subjunctive. *Maybe if I'd known it was this easy, I would have started years ago.* "Would have started": that's subjunctive. It's a possibility, not a promise. Everyone else has about a million questions, but it makes perfect sense to me.

The next day Señora Nelson wants to talk to me after class. This is becoming a pattern. I know it doesn't go this way for everyone, because I've seen classmates not turn in homework for as many years as I've been in school, and plenty of times the teacher seems fine with calling them out in front of everybody, in the middle of class. But with me, it's some big secret.

Like Mr. Bartlett, Señora Nelson is certain there must be a misunderstanding.

"I didn't see your worksheet yesterday," she says. "Are you sure you handed it in?"

She is giving me an out, I realize. So strong is her faith in my homework-doing that she'd sooner believe that she lost it than that I didn't do it. I could say, "Oh, yes, that's so weird," and she'd probably wave it off, tell me not to worry, to just redo it and hand it in when I can. She might even just give me the points for free. She trusts I would have gotten everything right.

"No," I say, a bit shakily. "I didn't."

"Oh!" she says. "Why not?"

"I just didn't do it," I say. "I'm sorry." I kick myself for that reflexive apology. At the same time, it's important to remember that this is a process. I can't expect myself to become great at giving up in just a few weeks.

"Oh!" she says again. "Can I ask why? I mean. Do you have questions?"

"No," I say. I'm regretting choosing Señora Nelson first. She likes me so much. I like her, too. "I don't really have an explanation."

I watch her think this over, and she watches me, waiting for some major confession to come rushing out. Part of me is waiting, too. But nothing comes. I look at my watch: I have to get to civics.

Or do I?

———

After Señora Nelson lets me go—no, after *I* let *myself* go—I walk to the girls' bathroom closest to the school's side entrance, which opens onto the parking lot. Other girls are rushing to reapply lip gloss and redo their ponytails before last period. I brush past them, enter the farthest stall from the door, and sit down on the toilet, pants fully on. I am very familiar with this stall, having hid in it most mornings during the first two months of freshman year, before Cara and I became good-enough friends to establish a morning-meetup routine. I've seen many eras of graffiti flourish and be painted over since. It's early in the year, so there isn't much here yet, but on the right wall near the bottom someone has written *Smoke weed erryday* in blue Bic.

This gives me an idea.

I tuck my legs up onto the seat and wait for the final bell to ring. Then I wait a little longer to make sure the bathroom is empty except for me. I pull a black pen out of my backpack and uncap it.

I think about what I could write on the wall that would impress whoever pees here next. It should be something funny or else profound. It should say something about how meaningless this all is, so that if some little freshman me comes in, she'll save herself the trouble. It should be dark but also inspiring.

I draw a tiny line, hoping something will come to me, but my pen is gel, and the ink smears across the rust-orange paint. I lick my thumb and try to wipe it off, but this just leaves an inky, smeared thumbprint.

Could that be traced back to me? I wonder, thinking of all the true-crime shows I've seen. To cover my tracks, I write over the smear the first letter I can think of: *A.* My average grade.

Now I've limited myself to *A* words. *Apple. Abracadabra. Algebra. Aaaaaaah.* I suppose I could write in all caps and put the *A* in the middle: *HAT. CAT. BAD.* I am up to the *F*-level vocabulary workbooks, but all I can think of are Dr. Seuss words.

There is nothing left to do but add a circle, making an unconvincing anarchy symbol.

I sigh, get up, and walk right out of school, fifty minutes early. Nobody stops me. I don't see a soul. I hustle down the front stairs and then catch myself, slow down. The key is to look like I'm not doing anything wrong. Anyone glancing out the window will simply assume I'm going home because I'm sick or have some other school-sanctioned excuse. I'm tempted to turn, to look up at the science-wing windows behind me, but I keep moving.

The sky is a brilliant, warm blue. Sometime between yesterday and this moment, the leaves started to fall. There is a breeze, making it just barely too cold for my jean jacket. Once I'm past the faculty spots, I'm home free. I breathe in: the air smells brand-new. I'm afraid and alive. I look around, half hoping that somehow my delinquency and Mitch's overlap, but I am totally alone in the sea of cars.

It's then that I realize I can't leave, not yet. The car my parents let me use—as they remind me whenever I accidentally call it *mine*—is also Peter's, in that it's my job to give him a ride home. I have to wait here.

Or I have to be here when he gets out.

I climb into the car, heart racing, and drive south till I hit the McDonald's. The woman working the drive-through asks me what I want, and I ask for a small vanilla cone, even though I really want an Oreo McFlurry. I pay for the cone with dusty quarters I dig out of the drink holder, and pull into a parking spot to eat it. It is the best-tasting ice cream I have ever had. I turn on the radio, and a song I like is just beginning. I imagine this is what being high must feel like. I could go anywhere. I could do anything. I have to drive back to school to pick up my little brother, but besides that, my life is all mine.

―――――

I consider calling in sick to work, because I'm on a roll and I don't want it to stop. But I need the money, and I'm supposed to train a new employee, and I make an extra dollar an hour when I'm training. Four whole extra dollars. Whatever will I do with them?

The new girl is tall—as tall as Jerry, which clearly makes him uncomfortable. She has super-short black hair that trails a bit long at the back of her neck—almost like a mullet but not quite. Somehow this works for her. She also has about nine ear piercings on her right ear alone, half a dozen braided friendship bracelets tied around her wrist, and nails painted neon orange. Her name tag, which she's decorated with shiny sharks from the sticker folder Jerry keeps in his office, reads ELYSE JHANG in tiny block handwriting. I like that she's included her last name. Most people don't do that.

As Jerry lists all the things he wants me to teach her, I appraise her, wondering whether we'll be friends. She's wearing a faded black polo I recognize as coming from the Target men's section, which I also tried at the beginning of my La Baguette journey. On me, a man's polo looked like a tunic. On her, it looks like what style influencers describe as "borrowed from the boys."

At the end of his spiel, Jerry hands Elyse an olive-green baseball cap with the La Baguette logo on the front, and he and I both watch as she reluctantly places it on her head.

"Can't have loose hair around food," says Jerry, half-apologetic, half-defensive. He knows how much we all hate the hats. He also knows we've all noticed that he, for some reason, is exempt from wearing one. As if managers can't lose hair.

Elyse and I exchange smirks as soon as Jerry turns away, and I get a little rush. It would be really nice to have another friend here, and especially one who actually likes me. But let's not get ahead of ourselves.

"Okay," I say. "Do you want to watch me do a couple transactions to get a sense of the *very* complicated procedure?"

She smiles. "Sure."

We wait for the lady hovering in front of the registers to stop studying the menu and commit. When she steps forward, I say, "Hi," and Elyse also says, "Hi," which makes me laugh.

"Hi," says the lady. "Can I get a half 'n' half with the Asian chicken salad and a turkey pesto sandwich?"

"Sure," I say, pressing the giant HALF 'N' HALF button on my register's order screen and scrolling until I find her selections. I shoot Elyse a look, like, *Get all that?*

She nods.

"Do you want a drink?"

"Just water."

"There are cups—" I start.

"—by the condiments. I know," she says. "Thanks."

I press CHECKOUT and give her the total, just under ten dollars. She pays in cash, and I hand her her change, her receipt, and a buzzer that will vibrate loudly and light up when her order is ready. She takes them wordlessly and marches away to claim her water cup.

"Voilà," I say to Elyse.

"She was friendly," she says.

"Oh, yeah, she loves it here." We smile.

"That seemed easy enough," Elyse says, then sighs.

"Yeah, sometimes people get really picky about toppings, but I'll show you what to do," I say. "Ninety-five percent of our customers just get standard half 'n' halfs."

"Shouldn't it be 'halves'?" she says.

I knew we were going to be friends.

———

Sophomore year I had this moron of a history teacher named Mr. Redmond. He was maybe a year out of college, and meaty, an obvious frat boy lost without his brothers. People liked him because he was easy: we hardly ever had homework, and he was impressed with even the most basic of insights.

One day he was teaching us about the Revolutionary War, which, like all wars, bored me to tears. But that day I couldn't *not* pay attention, because he kept saying—and writing, on the board—the word "calvary," when it was obvious he meant "cavalry," because that's what was written in our textbooks, and "calvary" means something else entirely. The first time, I chalked it up to misspeaking. The second time, I assumed I was hearing things. The third and fourth times, I wondered if this might be a very specific speech impediment, in which case it wasn't his fault.

After the fifth time, I thought maybe he just needed a re-minder. I invented a question and raised my hand. When he called on me, I said, "How did they decide how many *cav-al-ry* troopers belonged to each regiment?" Ingrid was in that class with me, and I remember her turning around to make grate-ful eye contact.

But Mr. Redmond didn't hear me, really. Over the course of his rambling, likely made-up answer, he said "calvary" six times or more, and then he kept on saying it, again and again, until the Revolutionary War was finally over.

It was the sort of thing that made you wonder if all the people in charge really deserve it, or if some of them got there by mistake.

———

It takes Cara a while to remember to ask me about boys, and Mitch specifically. This is just as well, because I have very little to report. I've seen Mitch exactly once since deciding to make him my bad-influence boyfriend. I was in the library, looking for books about low-wage work for civics, and I saw a puff of pink hair with headphones sitting at the computers. I was so shocked to see him not only in the building but in the *library* that I dropped one book and then another from the stack I was holding. I knelt down to retrieve them, waiting for him to rush over and help me, but he didn't hear me, probably because of the headphones. Even the people who did hear me just glanced over and then went back to whatever they were doing. Not that I can't pick up two books by myself, but the thought would have been nice.

I checked my books out and loitered for a bit, but this was before first period and I didn't have much time to spare. Eventually, I had to leave. Mitch showed no signs of having anywhere else to be.

I spent the next several hours daydreaming about him, replaying the same fantasy over and over. In it Mitch picks me up after school. I climb into his car—my hair is perfect, my clothes are vintage—and he turns and gives me a smile that would buckle my knees if I were still standing. Then we drive off together.

I don't know where we are going. I don't know what we will do when we get there. This part doesn't interest me. It's the very beginning, when everything starts to change, when I am *going*, that thrills me.

I don't tell Cara any of this when she finally asks for an update. My daydreams feel too private, even for her. I don't know if it's normal, the way I give myself butterflies just imagining that somebody likes me. I do tell her I saw him in the library before school, though, and boy, is she shocked.

"You have to go back," she says.

"Okay," I say. "I mean, I don't need anything else, though."

She gives me her *That's not the point* look. Which I know. Obviously. It's just that I feel weird walking into the library without a purpose. Or with the sole purpose of stalking.

"It's not *stalking*," says Cara. "It's *light recon*."

So the next day I try again. I tell Peter we have to leave early for school, and he's annoyed, but he doesn't have a driver's license and I do.

The school library is creepy and makes me think of Columbine. Though I guess a lot of things make me think of Columbine, and of school shootings in general. Everyone's always trying to figure out who it would be, if it's going to be anyone. A white boy who hates his ex-girlfriend, probably.

Daylight saving hasn't happened yet, so it's barely light out. The librarian, Brian, blinks wearily at his computer screen, taking sips of coffee from a mug that says LIBRARIES: WHERE SHH HAPPENS. Everything smells like dust and old paper, which I love. There are a few kids fidgeting in line for the printers, and a few more at the computers, frantically finishing things they will also need to print. Mitch is not among them. Relief floods my system. Disappointment, too, I realize.

But then I turn back through the E–F aisle to make my way out and he's there, sitting on the floor, drawing in a notebook. He looks up, and it's like I'm still twelve years old, smitten with nothing to say.

"Hey," he whispers. "Sorry, am I in your way?"

"Oh, no," I say. "I was just—" Here I pretend to scan the bookshelves and then zero in on a book I was searching for. I slide it off the rack and read the title. *Selected Writings*, Meister Eckhart. Sure, why not? I look at Mitch, but he's already returned to his drawing. I think of Josh. I drop to my knees.

"Hey," I whisper. "Do you know where I could buy drugs?"

Mitch blinks at me. "What?"

"Never mind," I say. I start to stand up, but he stops me.

"No, wait," he says. He releases my wrist, and it tingles where he touched it. "Why are you asking me that?"

It's hard to tell what he's emphasizing—that *I'm* asking for drugs or that I'm asking *him* for drugs. I don't know how to explain that I don't actually want any drugs, or know why I said that. *See, there's this guy on YouTube. . . .*

"I don't know," I say. "Ignore me."

"I don't do that stuff anymore," says Mitch.

"Okay." I pause. "Really?"

It's incredible to me that someone my age could have started and finished a drug problem when I haven't even tried a drug once. I am already so behind.

"Yeah," he says. "I'm sorry I can't help you."

"Oh, I don't— I didn't really mean it," I say.

Mitch raises an eyebrow. I can see the scar from where he pierced it freshman year.

I look at the book in my hand, announce that I don't need it after all, and put it back where it belongs. "Uh, bye," I add. I turn to leave before he can respond.

So that was one way to get his attention.

———

We have a new assistant manager at La Baguette. His name is Justin, and he's twenty years old. I was just getting used to the old assistant manager, Erik, but word is he got promoted to manage the other location across town.

"Justin is *hot*," says Kristy. I turn to get a better look, wondering what it is I missed. Justin stands with Jerry by the salad bar, hands on his hips. His corn-blond hair is gelled to stick straight out, horizontally, like an awning for his forehead. His mouth seems never to close all the way. I think Kristy must be confused by context, or that it's some kind of supply-and-demand issue.

"I guess," I say. I scan the dining room for Elyse and find her looking absolutely revolted as she uses a latex-gloved hand to scoop half a bowl of congealed chicken-and-wild-rice soup into the garbage. She's on dish duty while Kristy and I man the registers. I'm not officially training Elyse today—i.e., I'm not being paid for it—but Jerry made it clear that when I'm between customers, he expects me to show her what to do. As if collecting and washing the dishes holds a vast potential for error.

She passes by us with a bin full of plates and bowls and silverware, and I give her a sympathetic smile.

"People are disgusting," she whispers.

Don't I know it.

It soon becomes clear that Justin feels he has to lay down the law in this Wild West La Baguette. When I'm on my five-minute break in the back, eating broccoli cheddar soup from a teensy sample cup—which *everyone* who works here does—he spots me and asks, "Did you pay for that?"

I look at the cup and then back at him. Elyse, who's loading the dishwasher, pauses to glance between Justin and me. "No . . . ?"

"Store policy is fifty percent off your meal with a six-hour shift, and a free meal when you work eight," he says, glancing at Elyse. She resumes loading dishes. "How long are you here for today?"

"Five hours," I say. I know he knows that was the point. So I lift the last spoonful of soup to my mouth and drop the cup and spoon in the trash.

"Well, no more sampling," he says, less certain now.

"Understood," I say with a salute.

He runs his hand over the bread board, wiping nonexistent crumbs into the garbage, and then continues his big-boss-man loop around the restaurant. As soon as he's out of sight, Elyse and I erupt in hushed laughter.

"How *dare* you!" she says.

"I know," I say. "I don't know what got into me."

"Hunger?" offers Elyse.

I look both ways to make sure Justin's not coming around a corner, and move closer to the dishwasher and Elyse, just in case. "Kristy thinks he's hot," I whisper.

"Stop," says Elyse.

"I'm not joking," I say.

"But his hair."

"And face."

"And everything about him."

We're both nearly crying with suppressed laughter when Kristy pokes her head through the swinging doors. "Can you help me ring up?" she says. Reluctantly, I leave Elyse, and join Kristy up front.

Now that there's someone I like talking to at work, I'm irritated whenever work prevents us from talking. Every customer annoys me, even more than usual. First there's a guy who wants his sandwich without bread and can't understand how that might make it difficult to provide condiments. "Can't you just spread them between the layers of meat?" he says. (Kristy gags the moment his back is turned.) Then there's the group of women in a book club who come in once a month and always make a big deal about wanting to try something new before settling on the same things they order every time. Not one of them leaves a tip. When they clear out, there's a lull, and Kristy goes to sweep the bakery so she can talk to Justin, who's doing evening inventory of bagels and pastries. Elyse is out collecting dishes in the dining room again, and someone has to stand here. So I eavesdrop.

"C'mon," I hear Kristy say.

"No way," says Justin, in a way that suggests he doesn't totally mean it.

"Whatever," she says. "It's not like I don't have my own. I'm just broke."

"Hey, you and me both," says Justin.

Then they're both laughing for reasons I don't understand.

They're talking about cigarettes, I assume. I guess this is flirting. I guess this is what I'm supposed to be doing, too. I sigh so deeply Kristy hears me and asks me what's wrong. Actually, what she says is, "What's your problem?"

As if I know the answer to *that.*

I used to like school, didn't I? I used to be anxious on Sunday nights, not because the weekend was over but because the week was beginning and I couldn't wait. On weekends I didn't know what to do with myself. During the week I had a schedule, a plan, a place to be. I liked rifling through my dresser every night and picking something to wear based on the variable social and academic demands of the coming day. It was all so predictable. Despite most movies I'd seen, high school offered very few surprises. That was what I liked about it.

But, then, the reason this whole thing started is that I second-guessed myself. What if I only thought I liked school because everyone said I was good at it? Would I have liked it if I wasn't smart the right way or if my grades didn't matter? (Did they matter, really?) All that time I thought I did well because I wanted to, but what if I only did well because I was supposed to? Should those two things—desire and duty—feel different? What do I, Mary Davies, actually, independently, organically *want*?

I have no idea. Not one.

The first item on today's agenda is the student council inbox. This is where presidents can leave mail for their cabinet members, or where boyfriends and girlfriends, in theory, can leave us notes instead of using our lockers. Though the room is "ours," the door is unlocked, and anyone can get in. This is a policy Missy would like to change. At our Tuesday after-school meeting, she spends two or three minutes complaining about the riffraff she's seen in our space since last week.

"It's not safe," she's saying now. "What if someone leaves anthrax envelopes in our mailbox?"

"Mmm," says Ingrid. It's becoming increasingly obvious that Ingrid's greatest regret in life is asking Missy to be her running mate—which, I have to admit, does grant me a certain degree of schadenfreude.

"Why would anyone want to poison us?" I say. "We don't do anything."

Ingrid and Missy exchange a look. Philip stares at me, open-mouthed.

"That's not a very good attitude, Mary," says Ingrid.

Maybe it's not. But I've paid close attention to every council since I got here, and under every administration I see the same thing: a bright young star making big promises she'll never fulfill, because, ultimately, we are here to plan dances. Yes, in freshman year, I thought student council might teach me something meaningful about governance, but I was fourteen then. An infant.

"Sorry," I say. "I just think it's unlikely that we will be anthraxed."

"I like the open-door policy," says Philip. "It's democratic." He looks at me, and I smile. Philip rarely speaks, so to have his support is an unusual honor.

"I agree," says Ingrid. "I hear you, Missy, but our constituents have to feel like they can reach out to us."

Missy pulls a long strand of ash-brown hair in front of her face and plucks off one split end after another: *pop, pop.* I didn't know this was something you could do until I saw her do it, and now I catch myself doing it, too: searching the tips of my hair for little white dots and yanking them off like dandelion heads. The internet tells me this is not good for my hair, but Missy does it constantly, and her hair seems to grow six inches a month, and boys are always inventing reasons to touch it.

Anthrax aside, other items on today's agenda include a Homecoming-theme brainstorm and choosing a parking lottery winner. Every month, a student chosen "at random" is given the best spot in the lot, closest to the entrance of the school, which he or she is then free to use as of the first Monday of the next month. It's remarkable how often the winners are friends of the president or vice president. Next month's lucky parker is Missy's best friend Shannon's boyfriend.

"Okay, item two," says Ingrid excitedly. "I had an idea I think you guys will really like." She pauses for drama. "What about . . . *Candy Land*?"

Missy wrinkles her nose. "Like, the board game? That seems childish," she says. Ingrid's face flushes red, and I feel immediately sorry for her. "What about, like, *Arabian Nights*?"

"Um," says Philip.

"We can't do that," says Ingrid. "That's racist."

Missy frowns. "Like *Aladdin*?"

"Yeah," I say. "We can't do that."

"Okay. Well, I *don't* think the seniors will go for Candy Land. We need something sexy," says Missy.

The senior student council meets on Wednesdays, and whatever we come up with, Ingrid will bring to them like a cat with a dead mouse. In theory they are supposed to value our input, since we are also esteemed upperclassmen. In theory.

"It doesn't matter what we think," I say. "No matter what it is, the seniors will choose something else."

Everyone looks at me, then at each other. Even Philip is astonished.

"What's wrong with you?" asks Ingrid, surprising us both. "You're being such a buzzkill."

There is a long pause, long enough to hear the second hand tick on the clock above the classroom door. I liked Ingrid better as an impotent class rep.

"I am," I say. "I agree."

Ingrid softens. She seems to think I have apologized. It's what I would have expected me to do, too.

"Okay," she says. "I know it can be frustrating, feeling like the seniors are ultimately in charge, but if we come up with something really good, I think they'll listen."

Missy nods emphatically. We take a moment to think quietly about *themes*. What idea best lends itself to a six-hundred-dollar budget in a sad public high school gymnasium? Last year the theme was *Frozen*. There was even a very small ice sculpture of a tiger, our mascot. This cost $265.

"What about *A New Frontier?*" says Philip.

"What does that mean?" asks Ingrid.

"Like, space," says Philip. He is full of regret.

"No," say Ingrid and Missy and I, all at once. *Poor Philip.*

———

Forget a stray missed assignment. Forget the occasional, accidental B+. Forget spreading around my anti-efforts like seeds in a field of failure. It will take me years this way, and I only have two left. Less than two. Barely more than one and a half.

So I stop doing *all* my homework. I stop raising my hand in class, even when I know the answer and nobody else does. I start showing up late to class, and sometimes I don't go at all, and instead park myself in the anarchist's bathroom stall to scroll through my phone or read a book.

After three tardies in calculus, Mr. Bartlett tells me, sadly, he has no choice but to give me detention. He hands me a slip of paper I must take home to my parents for their signatures, acknowledging that I'll have to stay late the following day, and it's my own fault, and they will agree to not sue the school.

Never have I been so proud and so ashamed at the exact same time. Outraged, too. I feel everything at once, which is a nice change from feeling nothing at all.

At lunch I slide the detention slip across the table to Cara like a mob boss delivering a blackmail note. She looks at me weirdly until she unfolds it, and then she looks at me like I'm nuts.

"How did you even get this?" she asks.

Cara's new friend, Audrey, leans over her shoulder. This is a newish development I've been doing my best to ignore. Audrey Miller is pretty, tier B+ popular (she's on the dance team), and newly interested in being friends with Cara, which doesn't seem surprising or suspicious to Cara at all. Cara seems to think that she and Audrey were destined to be friends, actually. *Best* friends.

"Damn, Mary," says Audrey. "Did you get a B minus or something?"

It is clear from her expression that she believes she's delivered a very good joke. Even Cara looks a little embarrassed.

"Is that how you think detentions work?" I ask.

"No, but really," Cara interjects, "what did you do?"

"I was late." I shrug. "A few times."

"How?" Cara looks confused, which annoys me. I didn't mean for this to be a whole thing.

"I came into class after the bell rang," I deadpan.

Cara rolls her eyes and returns the slip. I fold it up and slide it into the back pocket of my jeans, feeling stupid for having shown it to her in the first place. What had I expected—a medal?

———

That night I give the slip to my parents at the dinner table. Mom's made meat loaf for us and some kind of greenish porridge for herself. When Peter sees the telltale slip, his eyes dart to mine, like this is some sort of trick. Which isn't entirely unfair. In middle school I once tried to prank my parents by bringing home a detention slip from my geography teacher on April 1. They were so immediately disappointed

and confused that I burst into tears, confessing my crime before I could carry it out.

"Is this a joke?" says my dad.

"No!" I exclaim. "No. Why would I do that again?"

"What happened?" says my mom. She lifts a spoonful of
sludge to her mouth and eats it, grimacing.

"I was late a few times," I say.

"Do you not have enough time to get to class? Did they change
passing time or something?" my dad asks.

I glance at Peter, but he avoids my look, relishing the freedom
of being left completely alone at family dinner. *Good for him,*
I think.

"No," I say. "Nothing changed."

"I don't understand," says my mom.

"You're grounded," says my dad.

There is a beat of shocked silence all around. "What does that
mean?" I say.

This has never happened to me before. I don't stay out past curfew. I rarely stay out *until* curfew. I drive to school and to work and occasionally to Cara's house. What can they take away from me?

My parents exchange a look, coming up with a punishment telepathically.

"No friends this weekend," says my dad. "And no phone when you're at home."

"For how long?" I ask.

"Until I say so," he replies. He points to the cabinet where my mom keeps a small Velcro pouch. Peter's phone is regularly confiscated when he doesn't turn something in and sequestered there. It's a tactic she saw on a blog: the Velcro is supposed to alert you if your kid is trying to spring his phone. She told us some of the moms even decorate them, but so far she has not gotten around to it.

I get up from the table and carefully slide my phone into the pouch while my family watches silently. For so long I lived in fear of this moment, and now that it's here, it mostly seems silly. Velcro jail without parole.

My parents sign the slip, and after washing my dishes, I retreat to my room. Without my phone, without my homework,

I am adrift, pacing the short distances between my desk and my dresser and my bed like a lunatic. Like the narrator in "The Yellow Wallpaper," that story we read last year in honors English. Not that I have it as bad as a nineteenth-century housewife whose quack-doctor husband is gaslighting her. But at least she had that interesting wallpaper to look at. I've got three dusty-pink walls and the one my mom let me paint orange when I was thirteen. I count up all the places where the orange seeps over the corner onto the pink, and pretend I, too, am being kept here by my husband. I pretend I'm dying of tuberculosis. I pretend I'm already dead, a ghost haunting the bedroom of the world's most boring girl.

———

On D-day, Peter takes the bus home and I navigate my way to the detention room, which is apparently a freshman English classroom I've never been in. There are little laminated quotes around the room: Shakespeare (three of them), Dickens, Fitzgerald, Wilde. There's one by Jane Austen, for diversity.

The detention supervisor is not a teacher but a principal's aide, with whom everyone but me seems well acquainted. Two senior boys stroll in, calling her by her first name—Jane—and she only pretends to be mad.

I pick a desk halfway back, not wanting to seem too sorry or too defiant. The seniors, clearly more practiced at being bad, sit all the way in the back. I feel self-conscious as they walk past me, but it soon becomes apparent that they neither notice nor care that I am here. Another girl rushes in moments later and takes the seat nearest the door. She looks like a freshman and starts chewing a piece of her hair. I had this fantasy that we might all become detention friends (?), but now that seems unlikely. We are not allowed to talk, Ms. Klepfer (Jane) reminds us, and we are not allowed to use our phones. She flies around the room, collecting them, and sets them in a stack on her desk. Our options are to do homework or sit in reflective silence. She doesn't care which.

I choose the latter. I think about the end of the world. According to the latest projections, I will be fifty when it happens, though I probably won't be among the first to die. As a middle-class American living in the Midwest, I am not at early risk for rising waters or hurricanes or earthquakes, but I have to assume tornadoes will also get worse, because why would one kind of natural disaster be exempt? I will have to make sure I am living somewhere with a basement.

The problem there is that when things start to really go downhill, all the people who live on the coasts will move inland, and there won't be enough housing for everyone. The rich people will buy everyone else out of their homes, and the rest of us will take the money and run. I imagine the RV business will do really well during this period, because the best option for most people might be to keep moving. We'll try to go to Canada, probably, but at some point they'll have to stop letting us in. We'll be stuck looping around the middle of a shrinking country, like those videos the news always shows of polar bears floating on hopelessly tiny chunks of ice. What if states break off like pieces of glacier? Colorado will be the new West Coast, and Indiana the new East. Goodbye, Oregon and California and maybe even Nevada. Goodbye, Georgia and Maine and both Carolinas.

But I'm being dumb. Obviously, it won't work like that. We all want to compare it to something we've already seen, but the world can only end once. We can only guess what might happen based on things that have happened before, but we haven't expected everything that has already happened. There is always the possibility of a totally unpredictable, unprecedented event.

Suddenly the English classroom smells like ass. Behind me one of the seniors smacks the other in the arm. "Dude!" he hisses, and I look over my shoulder to see him lift the collar of his shirt to cover his nose. I check the clock: seven minutes down, forty-five to go.

———

Most Saturdays I work a "close," which is listed on the schedule as from 2:00 p.m. to 10:00 p.m., though it's often later if the restaurant is busy and people are slobs, and it usually is and they usually are. My personal record is 11:13 p.m., otherwise known as "The Day a Kid Puked on the Fireplace." For some reason, in the center of the dining room, we have this weird little fireplace with glass walls on all sides, with a grate around it so nobody burns themselves and sues us. Why bother at all, you might ask, and the answer, I think, is that it's supposed to make La Baguette feel like home. If people wanted to feel like they were at home, I don't think they would come to a fast-casual eating establishment, but I am merely an associate and I've been told my decor opinions are irrelevant.

Anyway, the fireplace is surrounded on all sides by this really grainy gray brick, and one time, a kid threw up on it. The grate was easy enough to clean, but getting the puke out of every crevice in the bricks was nearly impossible, even after Jerry bought toothbrushes from the Target across the parking lot. For weeks afterward, if you stood in a certain part of the dining room, the barf smell lingered. Then it got hard to tell whether the smell was real or phantom, and that was arguably worse.

The goal for any reasonable closer is to start closing as early as possible without being caught doing closing-related activities, like too much sweeping or Windexing the glass bakery case of fingerprints. To "preserve the customer experience," Jerry doesn't want us to seem like we're rushing people out of the restaurant, which, by eight-forty-five, we are. The problem is that if we wait to start closing when we're actually closed, at nine, we'll be there till ten-thirty at least, and then Jerry will be mad about having to pay each of us our extra $2.25, or whatever it turns out to be.

But then there are perks to closing, too. One is that we can pillage the bakery for cookies and pastries and bagels before Jerry throws them out or bags them up for donation on the one day a month a charity truck comes by to pick them up. Having made myself sick on cherry Danishes and pumpkin muffins and double-chocolate-chip cookies, I now focus my efforts on procuring lemon-poppy-seed scones and oatmeal-chocolate-chip cookies—the former for driving to school with Peter, and the latter for Cara.

Another benefit is that when the frenzied nature of a weekend close doesn't make us all hate each other, it can be good for team bonding. And now, relatedly, Elyse works Saturday close, too. I'm just starting to worry she's quit and won't show up ever again when she bursts in at 2:02.

"You're late," says Justin, who is filling out one of his mystery forms on a clipboard behind the counter.

"Sorry," says Elyse. "There was an accident on ninety-four."

"You should leave early enough that traffic isn't an issue," replies Justin.

"Sorry," she says again.

He returns to his clipboard, and Elyse gives me a dark look that says something like, *So that's the type of day it's gonna be.*

In just a few short weeks we associates have become well acquainted with Justin's mercurial nature. One day he's chipper, everyone's best buddy, flirting with Kristy; and the next day he wants us all dead. The other week Kristy told me he's having "girlfriend problems," which doesn't exactly shock me, but knowing that hasn't made me more sympathetic the way it has for Kristy. I have to imagine that whatever problems he's having are mostly his fault.

When Justin's crabby, he gets obsessed with these little projects or guidelines he thinks will revolutionize the La Baguette business. Today, we learn, it's "add-ons."

"When someone gets a half 'n' half, you need to sell the add-on," he says, inexplicably impatient, like this isn't a concept he just came up with this morning. "Talk up the cookies. Add chips. Maybe a coffee. Don't just leave it at what they ask for."

So whenever he's within earshot, Elyse and I ask our customers if they'd like a cookie with that, or chips, or maybe a coffee, though it's 7:30 p.m., and the sun's been down for hours. Everyone says no thank you. When he's otherwise occupied, we leave people alone. La Baguette is not a venue where people come to be spontaneous, and I think if management just accepted that, we would all be a little bit happier.

Fortunately, Elyse has invented a new game to play between serving customers. It involves placing a plastic soda cup on the metal counter behind the registers, crumpling up pieces of receipt paper, and shooting them into the cup from farther and farther away. We call it "receiptball," and despite having shown no athletic skill ever before in my life, I am shockingly good at it. By close, I lead her, 19-11. It's all about the stance, I've decided. Even more motivating to me than the joy of winning is the way Elyse throws her head back and howls every time I sink the paper ball in the cup.

———

Something I think about a lot is the retreat my confirmation class took in eighth grade, the last big bonding activity we did together before becoming adults in the eyes of the Catholic Church. I was so excited I couldn't sleep the night before we left. Everyone knew someone who had gone to previous retreats and come home a changed person, immediately and irreversibly grown up. We talked about them like they glowed: real-life angels on Earth.

I had never gone to camp, so the retreat would be my first full weekend away from home, and I packed like I'd be gone for months, bringing three books (not including my junior study Bible), just in case. We climbed onto a decommissioned school bus and rode two and a half hours out of town, just far enough into the wilderness to feel the slightest sense of danger. Best of all, we'd been allowed to place roommate requests, and I'd been assigned to bunk with my best friend, Hanna Hughes.

But the retreat was about God, which undercut the sexiness. We'd all heard whispers of midnight hookups, but if anything like that *had* ever happened, our retreat leaders were intent never to let it happen again. The boys slept in an entirely different building, an insurmountable fifty yards away from the main building, where girls were bunked two to a room the size of a janitor's closet. Nothing about my life until that point had suggested I could count on a retreat hookup for myself, but I knew a number of girls (including Hanna) who were banking on having their first kiss at retreat, and I spent the first afternoon listening as my peers chose targets and formed strategies. Here was a social project that could sustain me well enough when group activities split Hanna and me from each other. If at a loss for other topics, I was always able to make friends with girls who were sad about boys.

When Hanna and I walked into our shared closet that first night, we found a mound of letters and candy and a trio of sunflowers arranged on Hanna's top bunk. She immediately broke down crying, rushing past me and up the ladder and into her pile. All down the corridor I could hear girls gasping and shrieking at their own bounties, and I ducked quickly into my bunk, where a single business envelope convalesced on my pillow. As Hanna cooed above me, I leaned over the edge to see if anything meant for me had fallen between the bed and the wall, but I found nothing.

This turned out to be the great secret tradition of the confirmation retreat: the leaders asked the parents to gather letters of encouragement and tokens of love from family and friends of the would-be confirmed, and then delivered them to our rooms while we cooked hot dogs around the firepit. We were sent to bed early, and everyone was annoyed, until we found what awaited us: a tiny, personal Christmas-in-April.

My letter was from my parents, or more accurately, written by my mom, and signed by them both. It was nice: they told me they missed me, they were proud of me, they loved me very much. I read it and I cried, as quietly and quickly as possible. Part of me hoped Hanna would hear me and climb down the ladder and ask me what was wrong, but she didn't. She fell asleep fast, exhausted by the love of her grandparents and sisters and stepbrothers and aunts and cousins. Hanna came from an enormous blended family that spent almost all their free time together, cooking out in the summer and holding basement potlucks in the winter. On the few occasions I'd been to her house for a big family gathering, I'd been overwhelmed and awed, her mom lightly teasing me for my timidity and refilling my plate when she knew I was too nervous to get up and do it myself. I loved spending time with them, but I was always grateful to get home to my own small, quiet family. I really was.

But I was jealous, too. The letters made tangible a deep loneliness I didn't feel particularly entitled to. I had two parents and a brother and a best friend who loved me. But I still felt so alone.

And that wasn't even the worst part of the retreat. The worst part of the retreat was the second and final night, the one that was supposed to change your life. After dinner, and after the sun went down, all forty-odd confirmation campers were led into a cozy, wood-paneled basement lit by dozens of white pillar candles arranged on shelves around the room. Anyone still talking to their friends went quiet. The head leader, a scruffy guy named Rick, took a seat on the floor and motioned for us to do the same. The floor was only thinly carpeted, and if I leaned too hard onto my right butt cheek, wood creaked beneath me.

For a long time we were silent, and then, just when it seemed like I might never again hear a human voice, Rick asked us to lift our heads and follow him in prayer. It was improvised—he spoke about our retreat in particular, but also about confirmation and Jesus in general—and when he'd run out of things to say, he told us we were each welcome to stand and *share a few words*, if we wanted. I didn't want. I was surprised how many people did. Hanna was the first one up, and within seconds she was crying, and wrapped up her speech quickly and vaguely. Then a boy I didn't know stood and talked about his relationship with Jesus, and other people started crying, too. After seven or eight people had stood up to talk, Rick told us he felt moved by the Spirit to lead us in song. He pulled out his phone and tapped the screen, and unseen speakers filled the room with a contemporary Christian variation on "How Great Is Our God." And then *everyone* was crying.

I remember looking around the room, stunned. *There is no way you all are for real*, I thought. *Some of you are clearly faking.* But it was dark, and hard to be sure. Later I would wonder which was worse: that some of my peers were fake-crying about God to fit in or that they sincerely felt something I didn't.

———

It's happened: I have my first C.

I thought this day would never come. After that first eighty-nine in physics, I got discouraged. I really did. I thought that maybe that was the worst I could do, no matter how hard I didn't try. But I kept on not trying. I kept on not showing up, not working. And now, halfway into the semester, I'm here.

I have a C in physics, and unless I start trying again—which I *won't*—that grade is unlikely to improve. God (un)willing, it might even get worse.

There are some people I should thank. Mr. Fullerton, for teaching an uninteresting subject in the least interesting way possible. I certainly would not be here without him.

Peter, for showing me what it means to not try.

Cara, for being willing to enable my failure so long as we continue to talk mostly about her.

And Mitch, for giving me something to not work *for,* even though he doesn't know it. Whenever I feel myself falling back on my old goody-two-shoes ways, I think of him, still somehow enrolled in school despite having done nothing for years on end. He is an inspiration.

When Mr. Fullerton gives me the news—holding me after class with that furrowed-brow look all the teachers give me lately—it is Mitch I want to tell first. For some reason I think that if he thinks I am cool and careless, I will believe it, too. I notice that even as I've gotten much better at failing, it still doesn't feel totally natural. I still feel like I'm playing a part, which I guess I am. But if I want it to *stop* being a part, and for this to really *be* me, what should I do differently? Everybody acts like getting good grades is so much work, but I've never been so exhausted in my life.

I need advice. I decide I'll get it from Mitch.

———

I find him—where else?—in the library a few days later, before school. He's at a computer, playing solitaire, and looks over when I sit down next to him.

"Hey, Mary," he says. I nod hello, and I notice he has recently re-dyed his hair pink: the dye bleeds onto patches of scalp around his hairline. I picture him rubbing Manic Panic into his hair over the bathroom sink, and I feel embarrassed. I hate to think of boys doing things like this: styling their hair, trying on clothes in a Gap dressing room, inspecting their zits in the mirror. Boys are so foreign to me that it's hard to envision them at home, doing the same strange human routines I do. One of the things that scares me about dating one someday is knowing I'd have to be around for some of that self-construction, and I'd have to find it cute instead of sad.

"Solitaire?" I say dumbly.

"Yeah," he says.

"Are you winning?"

"Hard to say."

I watch as he drags the three of spades onto the four of clubs and then turns over the nine of hearts. The cards on the screen do a very satisfying little shimmy when he clicks on them.

"Is the sound good?" I ask.

"What?"

I point to the cards.

"Oh, yeah," he says. "It's like—*thwp thwp thwp.*" He makes the sound with his mouth, his tongue flicking rapidly at his lips. I am momentarily stunned by his skillful impression (why do all boys know how to do sound effects?), and he laughs.

"That was really good," I say. "It sounded just like real cards."

"Thank you," he says. "I'm kind of impressed with my*self.*"

"You should be," I say, but it's one beat too many, and then we're just stuck here sitting over a dead conversation. Eventually, I realize I should also probably have a reason to be at a computer, so I log in to my email and print an assignment I won't ever do. I feel Mitch glancing at my screen. *This is it,* I think.

"Physics homework," I explain. "I haven't done any in a while. I have a C."

"That's not so bad," says Mitch.

"Well, for me it is," I huff.

"I guess so," he says. "So what happened?"

I've been laser-focused on my screen, but I turn to find him watching me, waiting for my answer. It's the same question I've gotten from most of my teachers, but when they ask it, they mean what happened to this one assignment or that exam. Mitch means what happened to *me.*

"I don't know," I answer.

He nods, but it's enough.

Now or never, I think. "Do you want to hang out after school?" I say.

He has returned to his game of solitaire, and he shrugs, like any of this is normal. "Sure."

Mitch and I decide to meet in the parking lot after school so he can follow me to my house, where I'll drop off Peter. When I get there, I pull into the garage and run inside to tell my mom I'm going to go study at a friend's house. She says fine but be home by dinner, which is five-thirty sharp.

I fly back out the door and climb into Mitch's ancient hatchback, which I'm unsurprised to find is a stick shift.

"Hey," I say.

"Hey," he says.

"I've gotta be back by five-thirty," I say. I look at the clock on his dash: it's 3:27.

"Not that we need to hang out for two hours," I add.

"Do you want to just drive around?" he asks, and I'm so relieved I almost shout *Yes!* My palms are hot and my heart is racing, but if we stay seated, facing the road and not each other, I can survive this, I think. And I love just driving around. To use my—no, *the*—car, I must always be going somewhere, to do something, but I often think about missing an exit on purpose, to see where I end up.

The stick shift makes all our normal suburban streets feel adventurous and new, as does the weird, spare, shrieky music that's coming from the speakers. "Who's this?" I ask, as if there's a chance I'll recognize the name. I don't, and I forget it immediately. Wolfhands? Snaketeeth? Some animal, some body part, something like that. They're not very good, but they're interesting, and sometimes that's better.

There are so many things I want Mitch to ask me, but he seems content just to drive and to listen to his music. He doesn't seem worried about what we're doing or where we're going or what will be said when he brings me back home, and this fascinates me. Maybe he often finds himself driving girls aimlessly around town in the afternoons. I decide I will ask him questions instead. First: "How are you never at school?"

"I am *always* at school," he says. "I'm in ALC."

This is news to me. ALC is the learning center where kids in our district who can't pass high school go. *Assholes' Last Chance*, people call it.

"What's that like?" I say.

"It's fine. I get to do more stuff I'm interested in."

"Like what?"

"Like shop. Woodworking and stuff," he says.

I remember this now: he was in my shop class in eighth grade, and that's where I first noticed him. When we made the wooden clocks in the shape of our state, his came out better than everyone's.

"You have so many unusual skills," I say.

He looks embarrassed. "Most people don't really see it that way, but thanks."

"Is that what you want to do—woodworking? For a job, I mean?"

"Maybe," he says. "It's a bit early."

In life, I think he means.

"I don't know what I want to be, either," I say. "Isn't it weird how we say it like that when we're only talking about what job we'll have?"

"Yeah," he says. "Capitalism, man." He smirks, and I can't quite tell if he's making fun of me. I guess these are things he's thought about before, but I feel that I am mid-epiphany at best, and it's unsettling.

Mitch pulls into my street a little after five, and the moment the car stops my seat belt is off and I'm opening the door, because I don't know what I want to happen now. He looks so unmoved and unsurprised by my hasty exit that I feel dumb for thinking anything might happen, here in my driveway at 5:09 p.m. on the first day we have ever hung out.

"Well," I say. "Thanks for driving me around."

"Anytime," says Mitch.

I spend the rest of the evening wondering if he means it.

———

"Please explain to me why you were in Mitch Kulikosky's car yesterday," Cara says first thing as she plunks down at our lunch table. Audrey, who had been hovering until Cara arrived because she wouldn't dream of sitting alone with me, collapses dramatically into the seat next to her. So now I guess I'll have to talk to her, too.

Cara acts all secretive about her source, and I make myself uninterested so as not to indulge her. Presumably someone saw us, and word got to her this morning. This is the first time that I have ever been aware of being the subject of gossip. It's not very good gossip, but it's a start.

"We were just hanging out," I say, willfully vague, both annoyed and pleased to be interrogated in this manner. Normally, I am the one doing the prying.

"How did that happen?" says Cara.

"I ran into him in the library, and I asked if he wanted to do something after school."

Audrey's mouth hangs open almost pornographically. *"Mitch?"* she says.

"Yeah," I say flatly.

"I can't say I'm not impressed," says Cara. "I didn't think you'd make it happen."

"Well, I don't know what you think 'it' is, but we're just friends," I say. *For now.*

"Mitch with the pink hair?" says Audrey.

I am beginning to think she has a problem of some kind.

"He's Mary's former *lover,*" says Cara.

"Ew, Cara."

"Isn't he addicted to meth or something?" asks Audrey.

"Not anymore," I say knowingly, though I have no idea if he was ever into meth. If I remember ninth-grade health class correctly, that's the one where you peel off your own skin because you think there are bugs in it. Where does anyone our age even meet anyone who knows how to get something like that in the first place? I guess I'll have to ask Mitch.

———

Tonight at work, Justin made Elyse cry. I guess her register was ten dollars off at the end of the night, which led Justin to essentially accuse her of stealing. I was mopping when she came out of the back looking so upset that I dropped the handle and rushed over. She thought she must have given someone change for a twenty-dollar bill when they actually gave her a ten, which means someone was essentially paid ten dollars to eat a half 'n' half, which is maybe how it should be. I told her it was okay, it can happen to anyone, but she said Justin told her that if it happened again he'd have to let her go. I told her there were worse punishments than no longer working at La Baguette. She laughed, but she was still upset. And that sealed it for me: Justin was my enemy, and he needed to be taken down.

So now I'm home, angrily chomping on a leftover poppy-seed scone, googling "ways to frame an assistant manager of a minor crime" in incognito mode. When I look up whether incognito mode actually prevents anyone from accessing your search terms, it's unclear, but I have to think it doesn't, because in the news they're always reporting that murderers were googling things like "how much rat poison for a human being" a few hours before their neighbor mysteriously turned up dead. In any case, my search is largely unhelpful. The internet's main advice? Talk to your HR department. As if La Baguette has one of those.

———

Soon, without paying much attention at all, I am riding around in Mitch's car two or three times a week after school. He texts me in the morning, or I text him: *Want to go for a drive after?* He never says no. I only say no if I have to get to work, in which case I say no, but what about tomorrow?

We visit different neighborhoods around town like tourists, naming the classmates who live in various houses, like they're celebrities. Once we almost get caught driving by Becky Villesvik's house, and I launch my seat back, screaming, *"Go! Go! Go!"* At that moment, watching him frantically struggle to shift gears, I think I might love him, or at least that I could start to. If this is what dating is, I could do it. He is easy to talk to, actually, and so long as we keep moving, there's always something to talk about.

It's when we stop that I have trouble. When I first climb into his car; when he parks in my driveway; sometimes even if a red light is long enough: I am hyper-aware of the distance between his body and mine, wondering if at any point he will do something to reduce it. I suppose it could just as easily be me— I'm a feminist, obviously—but there's never a time that seems right. My mom peeks out the living room window. Or he turns up the music. Or the traffic light turns green, and we go.

———

My mom has questions. She saves them for the morning, before the sun is up, while I eat peanut-butter toast at the kitchen table. She pretends she is busy, putting dishes away, moving things in cabinets around, but it's a ploy.

"Who's your friend?"

"Mitch Kulikosky," I say.

"Why does that name sound so familiar?"

"I don't know." *He was briefly my fake boyfriend in sixth grade,* I don't say.

"Are you interested in him?"

I groan. "Why do you have to say it like that?"

She rolls her eyes. "What should I say instead?"

"I don't know."

"You didn't answer the question," she says. On the place setting across from mine, in the spot where her plate would go, she has left a book splayed open, and when she's not looking, I reach over to lift the cover. *The Renewed Woman,* it's called. A thin blond woman stands beneath the title, smiling encouragingly. I let it drop.

"You need to tell us if you start dating someone." She watches me, waiting to see if I blush.

"I'm not."

"But if you do," she says.

––––––

"Everyone already thinks you're going out," Cara tells me days later at lunch.

Audrey makes a face that suggests she is skeptical about "everyone." Which makes two of us.

"I really doubt anyone cares but you," I say.

"Nuh-uh," she says. "There are plenty of girls with crushes on Mitch Kulikosky."

"That's true," says Audrey, even though she didn't know who Mitch Kulikosky was a month ago. I feel a frisson of something like jealousy. *Audrey, Audrey, Audrey, Audreeyyyy, I'm begging you, please don't take my man.*

The phrase "my boyfriend" rolls around my brain like a marble I can't quite grab onto. I want to hold it in my hand, in my mouth. Something true and embarrassing is that I sometimes say it to myself in the shower, like I'm introducing him. "Oh, hey," I say, softly, so Peter won't hear me out in the hallway. "This is my boyfriend." I love the way it sounds, the way the word "boy" bounces as it bumps into "friend." I love the stake it claims: my, my, my. What am I doing this weekend? Hanging out with my boyfriend. Whose sweatshirt is this? My boyfriend's. Is there something fundamentally wrong and unlovable about me? No—I have a boyfriend.

―――

In middle school we had this reading program called "AIR," for Advanced Independent Reading, in which books were assigned point values based on their difficulty and length. So you'd read a book, then take the corresponding quiz, and if you passed, you got the points. These were tracked by our teachers over the course of the school year, and as soon as you passed thirty points—the minimum required for the reading portion of our grade—you could start exchanging them for prizes.

Mostly these prizes had to do with reading and were therefore not very enticing to most of my classmates: there was a little night-reader you could clip onto a book, a jumbo novelty pencil, a piggy bank designed to look like the wardrobe from *The Lion, the Witch and the Wardrobe*—things like that. I spent all of seventh grade reading the longest, most difficult books I could handle (*The* Freaking *Mists of Avalon,* for instance: 876 pages, 25 points) and finished the year with a total of 211 points, the highest in my class.

The system had a fatal flaw, and it was only a matter of time before someone found it. Technically, you could take any quiz you wanted, whether or not you'd read the book. The quizzes weren't easy, and you needed eighty percent to pass, but some people were lucky, and some people read summaries and trivia online. The teachers eventually got wise and dispensed with the point system for the year, vowing to fulfill one last prize order before they cut us off. But my teacher never made that last order. She said she did, but she couldn't have, because weeks went by, and my Sherlock Holmes bookends (210 points) never showed up.

I think about the prize I didn't receive every time I see book-ends in a doctor's waiting room or at a friend's house or on sale at Kohl's. I think of my prize every time I hear the name Sherlock Holmes. These things happen more often than you might expect. I expect to be mad about this for the rest of my life.

———

Señora Nelson wants to talk. She gives me two options: after school or during lunch. I know I could refuse, telling her she can't keep me during non-class hours without reason, but I don't want to deal with the hassle, and among the teachers I'm disappointing she is the one I like most. So I agree to eat my cold lunch in her classroom, like a person with no friends.

"Have a seat," says Señora Nelson, and my instinct is to take *my* seat, though that would be weird with no one else there. So I move closer to her desk and take the seat I think of as belonging to Pepito, also known as Tyler Burke. Señora Nelson pulls a Tupperware salad from somewhere underneath her desk and opens another, smaller plastic container of dressing and dumps it in. It is mystifying to watch her eat. I reluctantly take a bite of my peanut butter and jelly sandwich and watch her stab her fork into the plastic container again and again, like there's something still alive in there. She takes a big, crunchy bite, and says, "So."

Here it becomes evident that I'm supposed to start explaining myself. *If I knew how to do that,* I think, *I wouldn't be here.*

"I don't know what you want me to say." *I have made a mistake,* I think. With another teacher I could lean into my dislike, but seeing Señora Nelson look so concerned makes me want to cry. I can't help it.

"You don't have to say anything in particular," she says. "But obviously, something is going on with you."

My sandwich feels like cement in my mouth. I feel envious of Señora's crisp, slippery salad. Salad would have been easier in this situation. I swallow hard and take a long drink of water.

"Just because I don't have an A doesn't mean something's wrong," I say.

"I mean, that literally *is* what it means," she says. "And I can't help but feel responsible."

"It doesn't have anything to do with you," I say.

She takes another crunchy bite, looking skeptical. She really thinks this is about her. She might even prefer it.

I press on. "Do you feel that way about the other students who have C's, or just me?"

"My approach with other students isn't really your business," she says.

She has me there.

"I don't want you to feel like a bad teacher. Because you're not," I say. "I'm doing this in all my classes." *Ugh.*

Señora stops chewing. "Doing what?"

I didn't really want to get into a whole thing, but now we're here, and there are twenty-seven minutes of lunch left and I'm not sure what else to say.

"I just mean that . . . what you said about you and other students. This is like that for me. It's my business."

She nods slowly. "So you're not doing as well as you can do . . . on purpose."

Well, I think, *it sounds stupid when you say it like that.*

"I'm doing what I need to do so I can do what I want to do," I say. I am not entirely sure where this comes from, but I also think it's true.

"What do you want to do?" she asks. She is genuinely curious, which breaks my heart. I figure she wants me to say I want to be a Spanish teacher, just like her. Or maybe a writer, or a doctor, or a lawyer, or a social worker, or an accountant. Something that only takes one word to describe, immediately obvious in value.

But I don't know what I want to do. I only know what I *don't* want to do, where I *don't* want to go, who I *don't* want to be.

"I don't know," I say, and Señora Nelson nods slowly.

———

The customers are in rare form at La Baguette today. I have had two—two!—people ask me if they can get a half 'n' half "but with a full-size salad." Both times I explain that they are welcome to order a full-size salad but that we do not sell half a sandwich on its own, and both times they ask why not. I do not know the answer to this question. I tell them we just don't.

Later someone I'd checked out returns to the counter to say she was given the wrong salad: the Asian chicken instead of the Greek. She waits while I hand her tray to Dax, the guy working food assembly. He takes it and asks me what she was supposed to get, and she says, again, *"Greek."* We pretend not to notice that she's eaten all but two bites of the Asian chicken she absolutely ordered, and Dax prepares her a half Greek salad, which she takes without thanks. It'd be one thing if she was genuinely hungry, or poor, but she's wearing real Ugg boots and a Canada Goose jacket, and those cost $900. These are thoughts I immediately feel bad for having.

Thank God—as always—for Elyse. She and I work the registers while Kristy works the bakery side, doing almost nothing except selling the occasional triple-chocolate cookie or semi-stale slice of brownie pie. Between customers, Elyse and I discuss my belief that something is going on between Kristy and Justin, which is disgusting for a number of reasons. When he thinks no one is looking, he swats her lower back—almost but not quite her butt—with a cleaning rag, or a stack of applications. Whatever is handy.

"He's so freaking *smug*," I whisper when he's out of earshot. I keep picturing Elyse's face when he made her cry, filling myself up with hot rage.

"Mmm-*hmm*," says Elyse, snickering at my choice of words.

"Don't make fun of me," I say.

She holds a hand over her mouth and nods. I laugh a little, too, because of her *face*. When we've calmed ourselves, I ask her if she thinks I should talk to Jerry about Justin.

Elyse considers this for a moment. "And say what, though?"

I know she's right. I could go to Jerry and tell him I think something inappropriate is happening, but I don't have proof. Justin would get a warning, and then he'd make my life at La Baguette more miserable than it already is, and Kristy would for sure stop talking to me, and none of that will accomplish what I want, which is justice. Later, when a customer orders a frosted cookie with their dinner and I have to go get it, I try to get confirmation from Kristy herself, but it's clear she relishes the intrigue too much to tell me anything.

"He's obviously flirting with you," I say.

"He's a dumbass," she says. She is so pleased with herself, so assured, so above my childish curiosity. I could smack her.

As soon as we close and Jerry locks the door, everyone but me and Elyse—Jerry, Justin, Dax, Kristy—disappears out the back door to smoke, and for a few moments I freeze. I consider proceeding as usual, starting my way down the closer's checklist while Elyse and I enjoy (or at least while *I* enjoy) our brief time alone, together, without our horrible coworkers. Elyse makes her way into the dining room to start cleaning. I should follow her. But I can't do it. It isn't fair that the smokers get a break before they even start. It isn't fair that Justin can make one teenage girl cry and hit on another just because he's an assistant manager. It isn't fair that I'm still so afraid of a God I'm not sure I believe in that I say "freaking" instead of "fucking" like a normal person. It isn't fair that Hanna stopped talking to me or that Cara is suddenly best friends with Audrey Miller.

"I'll be right back," I say to Elyse, who is mid-schlep with the first empty coffee keg of four. "Sorry."

"You're fine," she says.

So then I'm walking, propelled by a dare I make against myself. Soon I'm out the back door and it's too late to retreat. Jerry and Justin and Dax and Kristy all turn to look at me, confused and surprised.

"What's wrong?" says Jerry. He thinks there's a   or something.

"Nothing," I say. "Smoke break."

Justin and Kristy both laugh, and if I could, I'd evapora them where they stand. "When did you start smoking?" say Kristy.

"Yesterday," I say.

"You should stop," says Justin, taking a long drag, thinking he looks so cool.

I fumble around in my jacket pockets like I'm going to find a pack I didn't know about, but then Dax pulls a cigarette from his, lights it, and hands it to me. I am floored by this kindness. He's vaguely handsome in a dirtbag-ish way, scruffy, ten years older than me, at least, and has ignored me completely until this moment. But right now I am in love with him.

I inhale until my throat burns and blow smoke into the cold night air. I feel certain that everyone is waiting for me to cough. But I don't. I blow it all out, and I suck it in, and I blow out again. I imagine my lungs turning black. Everyone finishes before me, and for almost a minute I am out there alone, thinking I can do anything.

When I get back to the dining room, carrying a broom and pan, Elyse greets me with a smile. She's wiping down tables with a damp rag. "You smoke now, huh?"

"Well," I say. My voice catches, and I pause to clear my throat. "Maybe just the once."

Elyse moves on to the next booth, swiping crumbs onto the floor so I can sweep them up. "Did I ever tell you I was in an anti-vaping ad?"

"*What?*"

"Yeah," she says. She turns to face me, suddenly concerned. She places her hand on my arm reassuringly. "I'm not saying that to make you feel bad. You just reminded me, and it's so embarrassing, for me."

Just as I find myself sort of leaning into her hand, she drops it. I quickly resume dragging the broom's frayed bristles over the carpet. "How did that even happen?"

"I was googling 'how to quit Juul' and saw a casting call," she says. "They wanted Asian American teenagers who couldn't stop vaping, and I was, like, 'That's me!'" She puts a hand on her hip and whirls the dishrag around like a hanky. "I got three hundred bucks!"

"Wow," I say. "That's like . . . thirty half 'n' halfs!"

Elyse laughs hard, and I think, *If I do die of lung cancer, it will have been worth it, for this.*

————

It's a Wednesday in December, and Mitch and I are driving around in a gated neighborhood that encircles its own lake like a reverse moat. Technically, you aren't supposed to enter a gated neighborhood unless you live there or are visiting someone who does, but we both know people we could claim to be visiting if the gated neighborhood's private security guards were to pull us over. Audrey Miller lives here, for instance. Not that I've been to her house, but Cara has. She is probably there now, doing whatever it is they do when they hang out after school. One time I asked her what they do together, and she looked at me like it was the dumbest question she had ever heard. The implication, I guess, was that they do the same kinds of things Cara and I do when we hang out. But I have a hard time picturing Audrey Miller trying to teach herself YouTube choreography or painting her toenails ten different colors while watching a kids' movie for the fifteenth time. Not that we do that so much anymore.

I suppose Cara and Audrey just talk, and probably about boys. Audrey and her boyfriend, Nic, break up at least once a quarter, and between the breakups the drama is constant. Lately, even when Audrey isn't around and it's just Cara and me, we talk mostly about Nic and the most recent thing he's done to prove himself undeserving. These include: not texting her back for two full hours on a day she knows he was home; talking to Cammie Perez too much at a party; failing to ask her to Homecoming in an original or even half-assedly creative way; etc. This is what having a boyfriend is, and I want one anyway, because then at least the problems I'm always talking about would be mine.

Mitch asks me what I'm thinking about, but somehow I don't think he'll care about Audrey Miller's boyfriend or understand the havoc he's wreaked on my friendship with Cara, so I lie and say I'm thinking about aliens, the first thing that comes to mind, as they are always hovering nearby in my brain. This answer makes Mitch laugh.

"What about them?" he says.

"I guess I feel a little sorry for them," I say.

He laughs again, a kind of squawk. Something I like about talking to Mitch is that I often find myself saying things I didn't know I thought until I say them. Either I am a lot more entertaining than I've been led to believe or he finds me more entertaining than anyone else I've ever met.

"It's true," I go on. "I feel like they're trying so hard to get our attention and nobody cares."

"People care," says Mitch. "There are, like, a million movies about them."

"Yeah—our made-up version of them, where they're all huge and ugly and evil!"

"As opposed to what they really look like," says Mitch.

"They probably don't look like anything we can even picture," I say. "They probably have extra dimensions we can't see."

"Hmm," says Mitch. "I kind of prefer the reptilian model."

I groan. I am disgusted.

"What??" he asks.

"I hate the reptilians. I do not want to see a gecko the size of a person. It's wrong."

"I like the pictures online where it's 'proof' the president is a reptilian because he's got a wrinkle at his temple or whatever," Mitch says.

I have not seen these pictures, so he tells me what to search for on my phone, and I scroll through them, laughing. I can tell he's proud to have shown me something new and funny. He looks over to see what I'm seeing, and I look back, and he smiles, and something changes in the atmosphere of this car. All at once, I am certain: he likes me.

I am quiet, too quiet, until Mitch drops me off, but he doesn't seem to notice that I'm going through an inexplicable crisis. He talks about the cabinet he's been working on and the road trip he wants to take from one end of California to the other and the new speaker system he's saving up to get with the money he makes doing yard work for his woodworking teacher and that teacher's neighbors. When he pulls into my driveway, it's 5:23. We've been getting closer and closer to my dinner curfew as the weeks go by. He shifts the car into neutral, and he looks at me, and there is an unmistakable Moment.

A *moment* is that part in a romantic comedy when the two main characters see each other differently, or one of them does, and time stops, and you at home are gripping your seat, screaming, *Kiss! Kiss!* You at home are never thinking, *Well, what if they're not really a good match?* or *What if his play-boy ways really don't change?* or *What if she's been single all this time because her job really is the most important thing to her and what's so bad about that anyway, if that's what she likes?* You're not thinking about what happens next, how their lives will or won't fit together, or the fights they are bound to have. You're thinking, *This is what I've been waiting for. This is a new beginning, and it's also the end, as far as I'm concerned.*

I watch these movies, and I physically ache. I replay the scenes, with me transposed in the part of the girl, and I feel all the butterflies I'm supposed to feel in real life—the way I should feel right now. And I do feel nervous, and one could argue that nervous is a cousin of butterflies. *Maybe this is how it is in real life,* I think. I have no other *moments* to compare this one with.

"I should go," I find myself saying, both superfluously (because we are in my driveway for this very reason) and rudely (because it is clear that Mitch does not want me to go).

Mitch nods. "I keep thinking you'll invite me in for dinner one of these days," he says.

"Oh, I—" I start. But I have no way to finish. This has never occurred to me, and the fact that it's never occurred to me makes me feel like garbage.

"I'll see you tomorrow," he says.

I don't have the heart to tell him I can't drive around tomorrow, I have work. I'll save it for text.

Mitch looks at me, and there's another *moment*. Sixteen years without a single one, and now I've had two in one day. I don't know what else to do, so I reach across the console and give him a one-armed car hug. He smells so good, like mint plus boy.

He buries his head into my neck slightly, wraps his hand around the back of it. I recognize that the scene I'm in is sexy. If somebody else were playing me, it might end another way, but I pull back, I fake-smile, I get out of the car, and I go home.

———

I figure it's time for a check-in with Cara. I don't really want Audrey around to listen and judge me for my prudishness or lack of grace or whatever it is that made me act the way I did in Mitch's car, but I don't have much choice. What began as a casual lunchtime decision born of necessity—Audrey not having anyone cooler to sit with—has become a full-on affair. She hasn't said so to me explicitly, but I'm certain that if a neutral third party were to ask Cara who her best friend is, she would no longer say my name but Audrey's. If a neutral third party were to ask Audrey who *her* best friend was, she would say Naomi McNeel, because even though Audrey and Cara spend much more time together, Naomi McNeel is more popular. Who would Naomi McNeel choose? Lauren Oakley. On and on it goes up the social ladder until you get to AJ Pratt and Caroline Day, who are claimed by many but claim only each other.

You would think "best friendship" implies a degree of mutuality, or at least real experience, but I have learned that it is more of an avatar than anything else. "Best friend" is the person you most want associated with you, the person you'd elect as your social representative in the event of your incapacitation. Some of us are more delusional about that person's willingness than others.

Cara is still my best friend because I know no one better to take her place. Someday, I think, Elyse might belong there, but even thinking it embarrasses me. It's far too early, and to her I am likely only a coworker. But for a long time I didn't meet anybody I liked enough to even imagine that she might one day earn my "best friend" designation, and now I have, and that much feels good, even if that's all it ever is.

So anyway . . . I tell Cara and Audrey about the incident in the car.

"He absolutely wanted to kiss you," says Cara.

"You sure?" I say. I believe her, mostly, but I want to hear her say it again. *Tell me someone wanted me.*

"One hundred percent," she says. Even Audrey nods emphatically.

"Okay, but, he didn't," I say. I replay the scene in my mind, trying to pinpoint the moment *the moment* went wrong. But he could have leaned over anytime. He didn't try, and I say this again.

"Why didn't you kiss *him?*" asks Audrey. "Boys love girls who make the first move."

This is probably true for Audrey.

"I don't know," I say. "That didn't really occur to me."

"How is that possible?" says Cara.

I tell her I don't know.

"Whatever," says Audrey. "Next time you see him, you're definitely gonna make out."

"Whoa, whoa, whoa," I say. "Slow down."

Cara and Audrey exchange a look that says *Classic Mary,* and not in a nice way.

"Were you hoping for, like, a peck?" says Cara.

"It's just kissing," says Audrey.

Easy for them to say, I think. Like it's something you just fall into. Like all you have to do is want something to happen, and it does.

———

Oh, happy day: Kristy called out, and Elyse is here to sub for her. It is dead at La Baguette tonight, and Justin paces around, stressed and watching the door. "This is bad," he keeps saying, like a SWAT team is about to burst in—instead of what he's hoping for: bedraggled suburban parents with small children. If only.

Elyse and I split up the usual downtime tasks, and I volunteer for all the worst ones. She sweeps, and I wipe the counters and the grimy rubber that suctions the refrigerator doors. She refills the Pepto-pink hand soap in the bathrooms, and I Windex the door, knowing I'll have to do it again the minute someone walks in. Elyse restocks the biodegradable drink cups, and I go into the back to scoop ice from the machine into a water barrel with the top cut off. I haul it out to the floor and use a step stool so I can dump it into the top of the soda machine, wincing at the volume of the crashing ice. We do everything, truly everything, it is possible to do before closing, and by the time we're done it's barely seven-fifteen.

It's one of those rare days when I feel like it's virtuous to be here, helping in a roundabout way to keep this place going. I've been not-trying so hard at school that I'm finding I need somewhere to put some energy, and it might as well be here. My parents do not know this yet, but I currently have a 3.0. Finals are next week, and grades will be posted online before Christmas.

But I'm not thinking about school as much as I'm thinking about Mitch, which was sort of the point. It's increasingly impressive to me that anyone can have a boyfriend *and* get good grades, too. He's not even my boyfriend, but I think about him all the time, and he eats up six or eight hours of my would-be study hours every week. After talking to Cara (and, reluctantly, to Audrey), I feel even dumber about what happened or didn't happen yesterday in the car. I look over at Elyse, currently wiping down the bakery sneeze guard for the third time, and it occurs to me that she might know something that could help me, or at least make me feel a little better. She has the appearance of someone who knows about dating and sex, though maybe it's just the piercings.

A couple of college kids come in, sending the reindeer bell we have hanging on the door for the holiday season ringing. I glare at them, annoyed they interrupted my plan, but it soon becomes clear that they are profoundly stoned and totally helpless.

After no more than thirty seconds, the girl gasps. She wears fingerless gray gloves, and her curly red hair bursts from her neon-green beanie. "Oh my God, have we been taking forever?" she cries.

The boy, skinny and tall and shaggy, snickers. "It's been, like, two seconds, Ag," he says.

"You're fine," I reassure her, even though every second she takes up studying the menu is one second less I have to talk to Elyse.

The redhead looks over her shoulder, but no one is there. She and the boy murmur quietly to each other, weighing their options. I think they think I can't hear them, but I can.

"Okay, if I get the wild-rice bread bowl and you get the turkey sandwich and the Caesar salad, we can split all three," says the girl.

"Wait. Wait . . . ," says the boy. "Why don't we each get a half 'n' half? I'll get a turkey sandwich and a Caesar salad, and you can get a turkey sandwich and a wild-rice bread bowl."

"You can't get a bread bowl with a half 'n' half," the girl and I say in unison. She faces me, eyes wide, and bursts into laughter. Against my stronger instincts, I am charmed. I want to help these hungry, confused lovebirds.

"Tell you what," I say, waving them closer. "Do your half 'n' halfs, and I'll make sure you get a bread bowl."

They act as though I have just informed them they've won $10,000. *Thank you, thank you, thank you,* they coo. I ring it up like a regular soup, and then I tell Eric on assembly to swap in a bread bowl. He nods. He doesn't give a shit. I go to the bakery and grab a brownie that's gone crusty around the edges, and I give this to Eric to put on their tray, too.

After a minute or two, Eric calls out, "Agnes?" and they pick up their trays looking like kids on Christmas morning, oohing and aahing at the bounty. And I feel just like Santa. They are so happy because of something I did, and that makes me feel good. Better than I have in weeks, maybe. Is that sad or what?

I finally get my chance when we count our registers after the restaurant closes. This is always my favorite part, mainly because I get to sit down. I like counting the rough pa-pery bills like a rich person paying for expensive objects in cash: twenty, forty, sixty, eighty, one hundred. The coins are grimy always, but I like dropping them back in the drawer, counting, using simple math to get a total I can write down.

Tonight, though, I'm distracted. I mess up counting the nick-els and have to start over twice. I don't know how to broach the subject of boys with Elyse, and I sense something will change when I do.

Eventually, I just say it, vaulting the words from my lips. "I have a boy problem, and you seem like someone who might know what to do in a situation like that, so I was just wonder-ing if I could tell you about it and maybe you'd know what I should do," I sputter.

Elyse laughs. "Tell me. But I have to warn you, I'm no boy expert."

She is being modest, I think, which makes me like her more. Then she says, "I'm gay," by way of explanation, and my whole body goes clammy.

"*Oh,*" I say. "I'm so sorry. I mean, not that you're gay—that's great—but sorry I assumed you were straight."

Elyse shrugs. "So do most people."

I have never met a gay person before. Or at least not one who admits it. There are a couple boys at school whom everyone suspects.

Whatever I wanted to say about Mitch has been wiped clean from my brain, which now projects a neon sign proclaiming, *GAY?!?!* This is all I want to talk about now, but I don't want Elyse to feel like a zoo animal, so I try to curtail my obvious fascination and forcibly steer myself back to the subject of (how pedestrian) . . . boys.

"Well, now I feel dumb," I say.

"Don't!" says Elyse. "Let me hear it."

"Okay," I say. "Well," I start again. It is incredible how little I care, suddenly. Minutes ago I was dying to talk to Elyse and/ or anyone about what's going on with Mitch, and now I'm boring myself to sleep just thinking about it. Elyse looks at me expectantly.

"Basically, there's just this guy at school who I've been hanging out with a lot, and I think he likes me, but we haven't kissed or anything yet, so I'm not sure," I say. I feel nauseous. I sound twelve. "It's simple, at least according to my friend

Cara. She says I should just kiss him, but I don't know." I hear myself lower my voice for the word "kiss," like it's a swear word, and again I just want to die.

"Do you want to kiss him?" asks Elyse.

This should be an easy question to answer. I know this: I picture me kissing Mitch on a snowy street, to a swelling orchestra soundtrack, and I feel butterflies, which can only mean one thing.

"Yeah," I say. "I think I'm just nervous."

I did not plan to tell Elyse that I've never kissed anyone before, but now I've implied it. This is something only Cara knows, unless she's told Audrey, which I guess she probably has. But Elyse has just come out to me, and we are closer than we were ten minutes ago. I see Justin look over, and I resume digging into the drawer. Elyse follows suit.

"Well, I think you should take your time," says Elyse. "But it sounds like you really like him."

"I do," I say firmly. He is cute and funny and sweet and smart and different. He is a safe driver. He is always on time. He sends grammatically correct text messages. He is there if I want him . . . and I don't know why this terrifies me. I don't know why I wanted Elyse to tell me to run and never look back. I'm let down for no reason at all.

What else is new?

—

Señora Nelson asks to see me after class—just for a second, she says. I go to her desk, because I haven't yet figured out how to walk away when a teacher tells me to come closer. Is that even possible?

Señora Nelson watches over my shoulder until the last of my classmates has left the room, which I appreciate, especially when she says she thinks I should see the school guidance counselor.

I don't know how to respond, so I say nothing.

"I know that's, like, an annoying teacher thing to suggest, and I can't make you go, but I think you might find it helpful," she continues. She looks nervous, I realize. Almost like she isn't only a teacher but a person.

"I'll consider it," I say formally. I half mean it. It annoys me that the presumed solution to my newly poor academic performance is counseling, like there must be something wrong with me if I no longer want to do my homework. Like depression is the only tolerable explanation for having suddenly decided that everything is meaningless.

But I am also curious, I guess, about the wisdom a twenty-four-year-old counselor can offer me. Maybe she will be able to tell me my purpose in life. *Ha.*

"You can go during my class," suggests Señora Nelson, and that seals it.

"Deal," I say.

—————

The guidance counselor's name is Ms. Weber, but, like, the second thing she says to me is, "Call me Kelly." This is supposed to reassure me, make me feel that we are peers, but she is the one behind the desk, with her degrees framed behind her on the wall. She's the one who could tell the school what's wrong with me and they'd believe her. *I sound paranoid,* I think. But it's weird to be here during the school day, when I should be in Spanish, and I regret agreeing to do it as soon as I sit down. Walking to the office against the tide of other students made me feel like a snail inching into traffic.

Kelly offers me a bowl of candy, like I'm five. Still, I take a Snickers Mini.

"So, what's up?" says Kelly, and again I wish she were forty or fifty, so I could trust her. But then I remember I'm not doing that anymore: I'm no longer assuming that age has anything to do with intelligence. *Talk to an adult,* everyone always says. But what if the adult is stupid?

"I'm fine," I say. "It's just that Señora Nelson wanted me to come here, so I did."

Kelly nods, and unwraps a baby Twix from her bowl. She keeps nodding as she chews, looking not at me but somewhere off to the side, thinking what to say next, or else about how good the Twix is. I was between a Twix and the Snickers, and now I regret my choice.

"I'm actually going to trade this," I say, waving the little Snickers in the air.

She nods like, *Totally, I get it,* and hands me the bowl. I am relieved to see there is another Twix.

"Take as many as you want," says Kelly.

I take one, hesitate. Then I pick up the Snickers Mini again, feeling guilty for sending him back. *Him?*

"Do most people take something when they come in?" I ask. I'm suddenly worried this is a test and I've failed. Possibly twice.

"Oh, yeah," says Kelly. "Everyone likes candy."

I picture Audrey Miller coming in here, choosing a 3 Musketeers, incorrectly. I picture AJ Pratt picking one of the hard, sucky disks, maybe cinnamon. Not that I know that either of them has ever come in here, and probably they haven't, but it soothes me to imagine them having an urge as basic as taking candy that is offered.

"I have a couple questions I ask everyone who comes in," says Kelly. "Is that okay?"

"Sure," I say. I sit up a little straighter.

"Do you feel safe here at school?" she says.

Physically, I assume she means. "Yes," I say. *Emotionally? Not always.*

"Do you feel safe at home?" she says. She watches me carefully, and something in me crumbles, knowing there are people who say no, they don't.

"Yes," I say. "I don't have any real problems."

Kelly smiles, which is a relief.

"Do you think you're allowed to feel sad or upset only about certain things?"

"I never said I was sad," I say.

Ugh. *I'm being a brat.* "I'm just saying that nobody needs to worry about me," I add.

"So why do you think Ms. Nelson wanted you to come see me?" she says.

Señora, I think.

"Because I didn't do my homework a couple times," I say. "But I don't think she makes everyone who misses an assignment get counseling, so I'm not sure what she's thinking. I guess that I need 'guidance.'"

"Do you?" asks Kelly.

I think about this.

"Yes," I say. "But I'm not sure if I need it from you. No offense."

"None taken," she says.

———

I have a morning shift at La Baguette, working the bakery and coffee. I wake up at six, well before the sun rises. My mom is awake (as far as I can tell, she is always awake) and offers to make me breakfast, but it's too early for me to be hungry, so I grab a granola bar from the cupboard.

"Be careful," my mom tells me. "It's icy out there." No matter the time of day, no matter the season, my mom has something to say about road conditions. She is a nervous, impatient driver, and I tend to brush off most of what she says, but she's right, I soon realize. It *is* icy, and the roads glow a dull pewter under the streetlights. Though I am, by birthright, prepared to drive in harsh winter weather, I skid a little at the first stoplight, ending up five feet beyond where I intended to stop.

Fortunately, nobody else is on the roads at six-forty-five on a Saturday morning, and as the sun starts to come up, even my somewhat homely suburb looks beautiful. The new snow sparkles on the strip mall roofs, making the nail salons and mail centers and Chinese restaurants look like nail salons and mail centers and Chinese restaurants at the North Pole.

I decide to take the scenic route to work, which means skipping the freeway for a somewhat curvy backroad with a thirty-mile-per-hour speed limit. This, too, is beautiful. I pass a house with a yard filled end to end with inflatable Christmas figures: Santas, reindeer, snowmen, Snoopy in a sleigh. Then, toward the back, I notice a Frankenstein. I laugh, and crane my neck to look again, and then I'm sliding slowly, slowly off the road into a snow-filled ditch.

I come to a gentle stop and sit for a moment, trying to understand what has just happened. I put the car in park, unbuckle my seat belt, and get out, sinking immediately into a foot of snow, undisturbed until this moment. Cold seeps in from the top of my boots down to my feet as I plunge step by step up to the road. From there my car—*the* car—looks barely tilted. If the road is the x-axis, the car makes a twenty-degree angle, max. I have been in the mildest car accident ever recorded, and yet this is possibly the most exciting thing that's ever happened to me. My heart is racing so fast, but the good way, not like when I think I'm having a heart attack. I could be dead, but I'm not. What generally goes unnoticed I now feel acutely: I'm alive.

I'm looking at my phone, wondering what to do now (calling La Baguette somehow seems most urgent), when I hear someone coming down the road. It's a pickup truck. I watch it pass, its driver meeting my eye. He slows, turns left under the overpass, and then, to my surprise, he pulls a U-turn, looping back around toward me. I stand still, dumb, watching him inch forward, then back, then turn, then forward, the reverse again, lining up his back bumper with mine. Finally he parks and hops out.

"Need a hand?" he says.

"Yes," I say, disregarding everything I have ever been taught about strange men in isolated settings.

He nods, and pulls a rope and hook from the bed of his truck. I watch as he hooks his car to mine, gets back in the truck, and drives forward, pulling my car from the snowdrift like magic. It looks like someone simply dipped the front in snow.

The man climbs out of his truck, unhooks my car, and throws his gear back in the flatbed. "Okay?" he says, offering me a diagnostic thumbs-up. I have no choice but to return it.

"Yes," I say. "Thank you so much."

"No problem," he says, climbing into his seat. "Be careful, it's icy."

"I will," I say. I get back in my car and drive the remaining mile to work, feeling stupid and stupidly lucky. Only later, while making a seasonal peppermint mocha latte for a customer, do I realize it never once occurred to me, as I slid, to press on the brakes.

———

Mainly what it is, is that I'm tired of being afraid to feel bad. Kelly asked me to think about why I did homework and worked so hard in the first place, and when I told her it was because the homework was mandatory—that was the point—she shook her head and told me to think deeper. *Not everyone does things simply because they're told to,* she said. *So why do you?*

I found the question startling and think about it constantly. In the morning, brushing my teeth: Why am I doing this? *Because I'll feel bad all day if I don't. Well, that, and morning breath is disgusting.*

As I make my bed: Why am I doing this? *Because my mom will scold me if I don't.*

Everything I do—almost everything, anyway—I do to prevent a later guilt over not having done it. Sometimes I know where the guilt comes from: my parents or my teachers or the dentist or the law. But sometimes I can't figure it out. Sometimes I do things in such a specific way, so convinced that it's right, but I can't figure out where it comes from. Nobody told me I had to wake up at exactly 5:35, but I know that when I hit snooze (which I've only done twice in my life), I wake up feeling like the laziest scumbag on planet Earth. It passes soon enough when I complete the next available requirement, but the sting is acute, and apparently self-created.

Then I wonder: *Is it God?*

Surely, God, if He is real, has bigger things to worry about than my wake-up time, but if He didn't put these ideas in my head, I don't know where they came from, and that makes me feel crazy. I remember the first time I swore: a tiny, whispered *"Bitch,"* said about my mom when she wouldn't let me watch some TV show all my friends were watching. I thought of it as a test: Would God strike me down for violating two commandments (two and four) at once? Would my all-powerful, all-seeing mother hear me and throw me out? But no, nothing happened, except that I felt very bad.

It's not that I want to feel bad, but I wonder if it's possible to feel less bad if I stop treating *feeling bad* as the worst possible outcome to every situation. Am I making sense anymore? Did I ever? Sometimes I think this whole self-deterioration project is making me lose my mind. But then I think about trying to go back to the way things were, and I know it's impossible. I can't.

———

Cara is getting impatient with me, which isn't surprising, as I am also getting impatient with me. I have been driving around with Mitch for a month, or maybe it's five weeks now, and nothing has happened. Nothing that counts.

"I don't understand what the issue is," says Cara. We are at her house after school, the first time in weeks. I love being in her house. Her living room is huge, and the TV is enormous, and there's a little fridge by the built-in bar that's stocked with lime sparkling water, an acquired taste I start craving as soon as I walk in the door. Cara drinks four or five of them a day.

"You want a boyfriend, right?" she continues.

"Yes," I say. "Obviously."

"And you like Mitch?"

I nod.

"And he likes you." It is not a question for her, but for me?

"I think so," I say.

She flings her arms open, like, *What more proof do you need?*

"I mean," I say, "I don't know. . . . Sure. He probably does."

"Not 'probably,'" she says.

It's a weird kind of pleasurable torture, talking about Mitch with Cara. I hear me repeating myself, picking at all the same worries like scabs, and I think, *God, I'm annoying.* But then sometimes it feels like she says something revelatory, or I do, and all the dissection is worth it.

"So why haven't you kissed him?" says Cara. She has asked me this question 824 times.

"There's never been another *moment*," I say.

She cocks her head at me. "That's not a thing," she says. "Or it is, but you can't just wait for it. Sometimes you have to make one happen."

And there it is. I'm sure she's said some version of this to me eighteen hundred times or more, but whatever it is about this particular arrangement of words, it clicks with me in a way it never did before. I am awash in connection and clarity. It is hard to imagine that kissing could ever feel so good as this.

———

What I do is set myself an ultimatum, because I know that if I don't, it won't happen. But even then I think, *Well, the person in charge of the ultimatum is me,* and *Yes, if I fail to meet it, the guilt will be overwhelming,* but still, nobody else would have to know I failed, and that is simply too much leeway for me to allow re: the issue of boys. What I need is an enforcer. So I tell Cara: *I will kiss Mitch Kulikosky by Friday or you can kill me.*

It is incredible to me that there are people who can just do this without entire committees to advise them and hold them accountable. But there is not enough time in the day to assess what's wrong with me *and* kiss Mitch Kulikosky.

So here is how it happens.

I drop off Peter and get into Mitch's car. My heart is out of control, and when he isn't looking, I touch two fingers to my neck to measure my pulse, to make sure I still have one. It is slower than it feels, and I wonder if that in itself is a sign of some sort of condition. Mitch notices I'm distracted.

"What's up with you?" he says. "You haven't made a peep."

He can pull off saying things like this because he is so cute and so dangerous. I realize I still don't know anything about what drugs he has done.

"What drugs did you do?" I ask him.

He looks at me, stunned, then bursts into laughter. "Mary Davies, you are something else," he says.

I like it when he says my full name, which is something he does a lot.

"But really," I say. "I know that was random to you, but in my head there was a logical pathway. And I've always wondered."

"Weed," he says. "Shrooms. Acid, a few times."

"Wow," I breathe. I am profoundly scandalized. Weed is one thing—I know of at least ten girls who vape in the bathroom at school—but the others seem so serious and scary and adult.

I pause. "Did you really go to rehab?" This was the rumor. By some accounts, he'd gone twice, having been kicked out the first time. I'd always found this detail unbelievable.

"No," he says. "The thing about being easily bored is that I got over drugs as easily as I got into them."

I feel stupid for not having known that this was possible: that a person could try something illegal and not have their life ruined once.

"Do boys not read *Go Ask Alice*?" I ask.

He laughs again. "That book was written by a cop."

"What? No, it wasn't."

"Well, not a cop, but like a cop. It has the D.A.R.E. agenda. Some therapist made it up to scare kids," he says.

"Shut up," I say.

"It's true."

I pause. "The LSD peanuts . . . ?"

"Never happened," he says proudly.

"I can't believe this," I say. I found the book in the library the summer before eighth grade and have been feeling sad for Alice ever since. "That book really affected me."

"I'm sorry," says Mitch, and he does genuinely look a little sorry. "I mean, I'm sure it has some good points."

"'Don't do drugs or you'll die' is kind of the main one," I say.

"Aw," says Mitch. He puts a hand on my shoulder, and I tense up all the way down to my feet. Fortunately, he doesn't seem to notice. "I didn't mean to ruin your book."

"It's okay," I say. "I'm glad I found out now rather than later."

His hand leaves my shoulder and returns to the steering wheel. I can't look at him. I remember my ultimatum. My second-favorite McDonald's is just two miles up the road we're on now, so I ask him if we can stop.

"Of course," he says.

We're silent as he pulls into the parking lot and loops around to the empty drive-through. He turns to me, expecting me to say what I want, a cheeseburger or a soda or a McFlurry—that sounds really good, actually—and instead I force myself closer and closer until he looks at my mouth. I close my eyes, and we kiss. We're kissing. I am having my first kiss. In the drive-through, the car still in gear, on a cold Thursday afternoon. With Mitch Kulikosky. Just like I hoped.

I pull back, and we both laugh a little. Mitch looks around like he's trying to remember where he is.

"Okay," he says, "wait, did you want something—"

"Yes," I say. "I'll have an Oreo McFlurry." I can have anything and do anything I want.

I eat my ice cream. He drinks a Coke. We don't talk about it, but he is suddenly bursting with other things to say, about making things out of wood and funny things his dog does and a camping trip he is planning with some of his friends. I wonder if it's partly the caffeine, or if it's only the kiss that made him this way. Kissing *me*, in particular. Because I feel almost the opposite: sedated, calm. Relieved. I am happy and I'm proud, but I need time to think. More than anything, I can't wait to tell Cara. And maybe Elyse.

———

For all its many flaws, La Baguette provides the perfect place to think. When I am standing behind the register, waiting for a customer to order, or I'm sweeping or I'm restocking cups, my mind can wander, and my hands do their own thing, without my input. It's a very easy job, which is not the same thing as saying I'm good at it. Kristy is good at it. I am fine. I will never get fired, and I'll never be given more than an annual twenty-cent raise. I'll certainly never be promoted. This comforts me, and gives me freedom to focus on other things, like rewinding and replaying the mental movie of my kiss with Mitch to feel a little surge of butterflies. I'm like a rat, neglecting food and water to press the pleasure-stimulus lever over and over and over until I die. *Again! Again!*

Cara was proud of me, if not as proud as I thought she should be. She grabbed me by the shoulders when I told her and shook me a little, but then she was already on to what came next. Did we have *the talk*? When would we? We had to set up a real date, not in a car. Homecoming was history, but what about winter formal? When and where would we make our public debut as a couple?

It felt wrong that after achieving what I'd been meaning to achieve ever since I turned thirteen—kiss someone, anyone—I should immediately have to worry about the next step. Kissing was one thing, but I still couldn't imagine what it would look like for Mitch to be my boyfriend. I tried, in my head, to arrange the two of us in different settings, like paper dolls. At the mall, out to eat, at the movies. Wouldn't we run out of stuff to say? Wouldn't we get bored?

So every time my brain traveled down this route, I pressed the lever: us in the parking lot, getting closer, the slight smile, the kiss. *Butterflies.*

On top of all that, I can't seem to find the words to tell Elyse. It's not like I haven't had opportunities: La Baguette is a ghost town tonight, the customers kept home by a minus-twenty-five-degree windchill that will make getting in the car after this hell. Will the engine start or won't it?

Instead of Mitch, Elyse and I have talked about the social hierarchy at her school vs. mine (the cheerleaders are cool at hers, which I can't imagine); TV shows; the U.S. women's national soccer team (she is in love with Kelley O'Hara); whether any mac and cheese, including that served at La Baguette, can compare with Kraft (it can't); and finally, now, What happens when we die?

It starts when Elyse asks if I believe in heaven and hell because I'm Catholic. My shoulders tense up, which is annoying. I hate when I'm protective of things I don't even like.

"I'm not really Catholic," I say. "I was confirmed, but I don't like a lot of stuff about the church."

"If you're confirmed, you're Catholic," says Elyse. She's pretending to wipe clean the touchscreen menus on the other side of the counter from where I stand with a broom I'm not using unless Jerry comes into view. Even Justin has given up for the day, grouchily eating a turkey pesto sandwich alone in a booth, jabbing at his phone. Shania Twain plays over the speakers, sounding way too lively for the setting.

"I don't go to church," I say. "I have unsubscribed."

"I think it's more, like, you get the emails, but you delete them," says Elyse.

"Would you like me to try to get excommunicated?"

She laughs. "That would be pretty cool," she says.

"I don't believe in hell," I say. It's as if I've just decided this now. "Or if I do, I think it's here. I'm not sure about heaven, but if it exists, I think a lot of people are very wrong about how to get in."

"Do you think *I'd* get in?" she says. She watches me carefully, and regrettably I blush.

"I don't know you well enough yet," I reply, "but I certainly think you could." *What am I saying?*

Elyse laughs, and I feel calmed. "Well, it's not real, but thank you anyway."

Uh-oh, I think. *Don't do this.*

"How can you say that?" I say, doing it.

"What?"

"'It's not real.' How do you know?"

"Science," she says.

"You believe in astrology."

"As a joke."

"You said you don't date Geminis."

"Because they're insane," she says.

"That sounds serious to me," I say.

She squints at me. "Are you mad?"

I pretend to sweep under the counter to avoid making eye contact. "I'm not mad, I just hate that," I say.

"What?"

"Being sure there's no God is just as arrogant as being sure there is," I tell the floor. "Nobody knows that."

After a long while she says, "Maybe so. But the belief there's something better waiting keeps us from making it any better here."

She's put into words a frustration I've felt but never been able to articulate. And I hate her for it. I wanted to be right. I'm used to being right. When I try to talk to Cara about things like this, she tells me I'm right, when I know what she really means is, "I don't care."

I look up at Elyse to find her similarly flustered, so I say the only thing I'm sure will successfully shift the mood. "I kissed Mitch."

Her eyes go wide, and then she reaches across the counter to swat me with the rag she was using to dust. It catches me on the arm, and I make a note to wash that spot extra thoroughly in the shower. Someday those rags will breed the virus that ends the world.

"I can't believe you're only telling me now," says Elyse.

"I know," I say. "I mean, it's not a huge deal." I decide then that if Elyse hasn't deduced that this was my first kiss, I'm not going to confirm it for her.

"Of course it is," says Elyse. "Tell me everything."

So I tell her about the McDonald's drive-through and the way I leaned forward and the ice cream I bought just to have something to hold. I tell her about how talkative Mitch was after I kissed him, and how quiet I got. At this, she frowns.

"Not in a bad way," I explain. "I just needed time to process it. Or something."

"I understand that," she says. "But it was nice, right? The kiss?"

"Oh, yeah," I say. "I said that."

"Did you?"

"Yeah," I say, though now I'm not sure.

"Fireworks?" says Elyse.

I roll my eyes. "What does that even mean?"

Elyse shrugs. "Like—fireworks." She holds up her fists, explodes them.

"Yeah, but how do I know that your fireworks feel like mine? I can't get in your body—anyone's body—and they can't get in mine," I say.

"That's true . . . ," says Elyse. She is humoring me.

"Sorry," I say. "I think about this every time I go to the doctor and she asks me to rank my headaches on a pain scale from one to ten. How can I possibly answer that without knowing what ten feels like to her?"

"Just say eight, so they take you seriously."

"But what if someday I have a *real* eight, and it's so much worse than before, and nobody believes me, because they think I get eights all the time?"

Elyse smiles. "You are a very tightly wound individual," she says.

———

The biggest problem with not doing my homework anymore is all the time it leaves me to think. This fireworks thing, for instance: What the hell was that about?

I don't know what I expected when I finally kissed Mitch—maybe a parade?—but I know it was more than this. Cara and Elyse and even Audrey were happy for me, sure, but then they had five thousand questions. I should be grateful, because questions convey interest, and it would feel worse if they had nothing to say beyond "Cool, congrats." But somehow the questions feel mostly patronizing. Like they know everything just because they've kissed a few boys before. Or girls.

Everyone acts like hooking up makes you wise, but there are dozens upon dozens of people in my grade alone who provide strong evidence to the contrary. And yet, what do I keep going to my friends for, if not for advice, if not for the assumption that they know better than me what I should do next? I do want to be told exactly what to do. I just don't want them to act like I don't know what I'm doing.

I say this to Kelly the next time I see her, and she laughs.

"That sounds reasonable to me," she says.

I take a second Twix from her bowl. She's started putting out more of them, I think. "I guess I also give people advice about things I don't know, though," I say.

"Like what?"

"Like telling Audrey to break up with her boyfriend."

133

"Why do you think they should break up?"

"Because I'm sick of hearing about him."

Kelly smiles.

"And because she always seems happier when they're broken up," I say.

"That seems like a valuable insight," says Kelly.

"I think so, too, but she never listens."

Kelly nods. "I think people hear what they want to hear until they're ready to hear what they need to hear," she says.

We sit with this for a moment. It might be the smartest thing I have ever heard.

"I saw that on Instagram," she adds.

———

I can't figure out what's wrong, but something is.

Three months into my self-deterioration project and here is what I have to show for it:

- a 2.9 GPA (projected)
- disappointed parents (mostly projected)
- unimpressed best friend (not a change)
- kiss with bad boy, who is barely even bad anymore
- mandatory (okay: suggested) guidance-counselor visits
- bewilderment from teachers and fellow council members

For a while, my teachers kept trying to talk to me, but when I told them I was talking to Señora Nelson and the guidance counselor, they mostly backed off, except to cast what they obviously deem as meaningful looks my way during class. I can hardly blame them; I am disappointed in me also, although for different reasons.

I still feel mostly the same. Certainly, my peers treat me the same. It's not like I'm doing this to be cooler, but I did hope that as a result of the unrelated reasons for which I'm doing this, people might find me a little cooler. A little mysterious, at least. But not one person has appeared at my locker to ask me what my deal is. Nor have I heard even one good rumor about myself. Isn't Cara telling anyone about me and Mitch? But then: Do I really want her to? That would put the pressure on even more, and I can tell he wants to talk. I know this because he texted me and told me he wants to talk. *We're talking now,* I wrote.

You know what I mean, he wrote back.

I do and I don't.

Even though I've talked to Mitch plenty, have been talking to him regularly for months now, and honestly, too—not just easy stuff about him, like I've done with every crush I've ever had—I can't imagine having the conversation he wants to have. I know that if I sit down with him and he starts telling me that he likes me—the thing I've wanted a boy to say to me since when, birth?—I will freeze. Or flee. Or maybe, if things go really wrong, fight. In any case, it will be panic that informs me. And if he asks me to be his girlfriend, I am worried I will say no even when I mean to say yes. And I want to say yes. I should want to say yes.

I'm just scared. I'm scared about what we'll do together when we're not in a car, constantly moving. I'm scared about what people at school will say. I'm scared they won't say anything. I'm scared to let Mitch touch me anywhere south of my neck. I'm scared he'll touch my chest and what's there will be so disappointingly small he'll never touch it again. I'm scared he'll expect me to have sex with him. Of course he will. He has done it before—dozens of times, if rumors about him and that older girl who moved to Arizona are to be believed.

I'm scared of his penis. I hate even thinking the word. So embarrassing. So clinical. *This is why we say "dick,"* Cara says, but that word, in my mouth, sounds phony. No such thing could possibly exist. Until now I've mostly managed, when we're together, to forget it's in the car with us. But it's my understanding that, sooner or later, it will make itself known, and then it's my responsibility. I have done my homework, I've read the hand-job-advice Reddit threads, but it's hard to really see it happening. Though I guess you could say that about most things you haven't done before the first time you do them. Cara tells me you figure it out as you go. To me this sounds like a recipe for disaster.

I wish this wasn't my problem. I wish this wasn't my life. I wish I'd never gotten myself into this situation. *What "situation?"* Cara says.

———

I'm not sleeping. Or I am, but not enough, and almost never continuously. I am only aware of having slept each time I wake up to look at the time on my phone. Forty-five minutes here. Two hours there. Then suddenly it's 5:35. Again.

I try counting sheep. I have a hard time doing this with actual sheep—it seems chaotic and sad, and I worry about where they are going—so mine are cartoons, puffy like clouds with faces that float on and off the movie screen in my brain. Sometimes I get up to 137, even 162, before I give up. *How many sheep does a normal farm have?* I wonder.

When this doesn't work, I try counting backward from 100, the way they had me do when I got my tonsils out. I was so sure the anesthetic wouldn't work on me. That I would be the first person in history to be found totally resistant, un-put-down-able. There was too much going on in my head. I panicked at ninety-eight, told the nurse it wasn't working. She told me to keep going. I don't remember anything after ninety-seven. I woke up without tonsils and enjoyed two bliss-ful days alternately eating cherry Jello and vanilla ice cream, watching daytime TV.

Without anesthesia, I get past ninety-seven. I get to forty . . . thirty . . . sixteen. I give up and start again. The endeavor seems more plausible in the nineties and eighties. Who falls asleep between twenty-nine and twenty-eight?

Sometimes, if it's really bad, I put in my earbuds and listen to a boring audiobook on my phone—the most boring choice among whatever is free on my app. Something about eco-nomics or politics or a novel about many generations of one family in the American South, their interweaving tales of love and loss. One time I accidentally got too invested in one of the novels and stayed up listening for two hours before turn-ing it off. Another time I downloaded a romance novel that turned out to be basically porn, which kept me up in a dif-ferent way. Now, masturbating—that put me right out. The downside was feeling like a little freak, scurrying into my creep cave to listen to vampire sex and hump my own hand until I pass out. Surely life was meant to be more elegant than this.

When I do fall asleep, I dream about school, always. I am back in middle school, often shirtless, struggling to walk, my legs weak and collapsing under me as I drag myself from one class to the next, trying to cover my bare chest with the stack of textbooks in my arms. Or I'm in high school, but it's not my high school, and my locker has moved and I don't know the combination, and I'm not wearing shoes. Sometimes I hear that there is a shooter, and I take off running in exactly the wrong direction.

I notice that I never dream about Mitch, and this, like so much else, worries me.

———

Just before the council meeting, Ingrid marches up to me at the mailbox (empty) and shouts, "You're going out with *Mitch Kulikosky?*"

Her tone is distinctly concerned, disapproving.

I smile. *Finally.* "Well . . . ," I say.

"Omigod!" says Missy. She has arrived just in time. I turn and see Philip, too, sitting at the table, hands folded across his treasurer's notebook, eavesdropping.

"I just said 'Well,'" I say, joining Philip at the table.

"Yeah, but clearly you are," says Missy.

"Mary, he does meth," says Ingrid.

"He doesn't do meth," I say. "He doesn't do any drugs now, actually."

"Wow," says Missy. "You're in love with Mitch Kulikosky."

"I am not in *love*," I say. It's easy to say and plainly true, which is a little disappointing.

"What's going on with you?" says Ingrid. She means globally.

I've been expecting this. I look at the three sets of eyes watching me, waiting for answers.

"I think I quit," I say.

"What?"

"Yeah," I say. I push myself back from the table. This feels right. "I quit."

"Can she do that?" asks Missy.

"No," says Ingrid.

"Uh, yes, I can," I say. I stand up. Apparently, I am really doing this.

"We need a secretary," says Ingrid. I notice she does not say: we need *you*.

"Have a special election," I say. "But I'm done."

I look at Philip, whose eyes plead: *Don't leave me here with them.*

"Sorry, Philip," I say, and then I leave.

I walk through the halls, heart hammering, and out the front doors. I sit on the front steps and wonder what to do now. Peter has taken the bus home because it's council day. Mitch has probably already left. I could text him, but I'm not sure what to say. I pull out my phone and scroll through my texts until I land on Elyse. The last text she sent me reads: *MY HERO!* [kiss emoji] [prayer hands] [turtle, for some reason]. She'd asked me to cover a shift for her, and I'd agreed. That was last week.

I type: *I just quit student council.* Delete, delete.

I try again: *I just quit student council lol.* Ugh.

I tap on her name, and suddenly I'm calling her on the phone, like I'm her mom. The phone rings, and I hold it away from my head, like that might prevent her from picking up. But of course it doesn't.

"Hey!" she says.

I press the phone to my ear. "Hi!" I say. "It's Mary."

"Yes," she says. "I know."

"I called you," I say. "I'm not sure why."

She laughs. "Well, we're here now."

"Yeah," I say. "I was trying to text you something, but everything I wrote sounded dumb. Not that I sound much better now."

"What did you want to say?" she asks. There is genuine curiosity in her voice, which of course makes me feel even dumber.

"Oh . . . just that I just quit student council," I say.

"Oh," says Elyse.

I close my eyes and wish myself dead. It doesn't work.

"What happened?"

"I'm not sure," I say. I pause. *I'm losing my mind,* I think. "Where are you? Do you want to do something?" I close my eyes again.

"Sure!" says Elyse. "Want to meet at the mall?"

She doesn't have to specify. I know she means the one between her suburb and mine, because that's what I was going to suggest, too.

"Perfect," I say. "Be there in twenty."

———

I park in the usual section, on the upper level by the entrance to Macy's. I don't shop at Macy's, but this is the best and least crowded parking lot among the mall's ten or twelve lots, by which I mean it's the one my mom uses whenever I come here with her. The stores we like are on the other end, but if you try to park over there, you'll have ended up so far from the doors you'll be tired by the time you get there, or you'll end up circling for four, five, even six full minutes before a spot opens up. My mom finds circling intolerable.

I find a prime-time parking spot and almost take a picture to send to my mom, but then there'd be questions about why

I'm at the mall and not at council, or studying, and who am I with, and can she meet me because there's a return she needs to make, etc. So I leave the perfect spot undocumented.

I heave open the doors to Macy's and speed past women's contemporary, hosiery, and the gleaming white Clinique counter, not wanting any saleslady to get the wrong idea. As I always do when in a store alone, I feel like a shoplifter, though I have never shoplifted. One time I picked up and kept an unopened pack of gum someone had dropped directly outside the door to a gas station, but I never opened it. It sat in the cupholder in my car for months. *Should shoplifting become part of my self-deterioration?* I wonder. Should I pocket something small, worth only ten or twenty dollars? Something nobody would miss, like a Victoria's Secret body spray? *No,* I decide. A sixteen-year-old white girl who shoplifts. What a cliché.

I pause by the fancy planner store to pull out my phone and text Elyse: *I'm here!*

Just parked! she replies immediately.

Which lot?

By Sephora.

I shake my head. *Amateur,* I think.

OK, I reply. *Meet you there.*

I pass Bath & Body Works, which stinks of Christmas; Eddie Bauer, where my mom buys clothes for my dad; Aerie, where I applied for a job (they never called) before being hired by La Baguette; Gap (ditto); Williams-Sonoma. I reach Sephora just as Elyse turns the corner from the other side. She smiles, and I wave.

"It's weird to see you not in a polo," she says.

I was just thinking the same thing about her. She is wearing Doc Martens and jeans and a black T-shirt with a shearling-lined jean jacket, and looks about a hundred times cooler and older than I do in my pilly blue sweater and knockoff Uggs.

"Thanks for coming," I say.

"Thanks for asking," says Elyse. "I wasn't sure if we were gonna be IRL friends or just work friends."

I like that Elyse says things like this out loud. "Me too," I say. "Or, me neither."

"I think I want to get a pretzel," she announces.

We take the escalator downstairs to Auntie Anne's, where Elyse orders a plain pretzel with mustard and I get a cinnamon sugar pretzel and a Diet Coke with a little bit of Cherry Coke mixed in. This is the order my mom and I used to share before she stopped eating bread and sugar, and stopped drinking pop. I haven't had Auntie Anne's in three years, and when I bite into the warm, sugar-crusted dough, I could cry.

Elyse and I sit at one of the stand's little tables, which is sticky and covered in straw wrappers. Now that we're still, I feel a bit panicked about having suggested this in the first place. I don't want her to regret having driven over to spend time with someone who doesn't have anything interesting to say. But she is taking huge, chomping bites of her pretzel, looking happy as can be. I wonder if maybe my first instinct shouldn't be to assume that I'm ruining everyone else's good time.

"This is perfect," says Elyse. "Lots of salt." She coughs, and I offer her my drink. "Mmmm," she says. "I'm going to start ordering this."

"It's good, right? It's like a more moderate Suicide," I say, referring to that thing where kids mix every fountain-soda flavor in the same cup.

"Those were so huge in fifth grade," says Elyse.

"For us, too!" I say. It's comforting to know the trend was so universal as to cross school districts.

"Not a great name, in retrospect," says Elyse.

"No," I agree. "Bit hyperbolic."

Elyse laughs and takes another sip of my drink. Which I guess is now our drink.

"Kids are weird," she says. "Remember when jawbreakers were a thing?"

"Also fifth grade." I nod. "Big year for sugar."

"Wow, trendsetters over here," says Elyse. "For us it was sixth grade."

"That makes me feel cool," I say.

"You should."

"My best friend for half that year was, like, one of the main dealers. Her sister worked at a candy store."

"Wow," says Elyse. "I'm impressed."

"Don't be. She deserted me at the peak of her reign."

"Bitch."

When we're done with our pretzels, we get up. I throw my trash away and turn to see Elyse still at the table, using a napkin to sweep it free of crumbs and wrappers. I'm embarrassed this never occurred to me. She finishes, throws her things away, and asks me where I want to go next. The truth is I don't care.

"Let's just walk," I say.

"Perfect."

We spend an hour and a half walking the mall from end to end. We stop in Bath & Body Works to smell the candles, making each other smell the worst ones we find. ("How is 'Midnight Stroll' a smell?" Elyse asks.) We walk into Hot Topic and guess what middle school kids would most want to buy to seem alt to their classmates. I point out a shirt with a circle cut out in the back, held in place by straps that form a pentagram. We are both surprised by how many shirts have Chucky on them, and wonder where the demand is coming from. I find myself picking things up just to get Elyse's reactions, which are theatrical and unselfconscious. Though we're here to make fun, I feel obliged to pretend I'm sincerely shopping, for the benefit of the skinny boy with blue hair behind the register. Elyse does not share this concern.

I meant to talk to her about Mitch, but I'm having such a nice time not talking or worrying about him that I decide it can wait. Of course, almost instantly she asks me about him. We've moved on to Nordstrom by now and are rifling through a sale rack in the most expensive section. I show her a lime-green sweater on sale for $619, down from $799. She wrinkles her nose, and I put it back.

"He's fine," I say finally. "I think. I've kind of been avoiding him."

"Completely?"

"I mean, we've texted. It hasn't been a week yet since we kissed," I say. "But he did say he wants to talk."

"That sounds like he wants to make it official," says Elyse. She pulls out a pair of silky black joggers with a white stripe down each leg.

"How much?"

She checks the tag. "Two-nineteen."

"I love them," I say.

"Me too," she says, and puts them back. "Why don't you want to talk to him?"

"It's not that I don't want to," I say. "I'm just nervous. I've never had a boyfriend before."

"Really?" says Elyse. Usually, when people say this to me it is with obvious, open pity. But Elyse is as matter-of-fact as if I've just told her I'm lactose-intolerant or afraid of snakes.

"Yeah," I say. "And I've had a crush on him for so long that I guess I worry it can't possibly live up to my imagination."

"Can I help you ladies find anything?" A woman with severe contouring and maroon hair appears at the sale rack, trying to look like she really wants to help.

"Just browsing," I say. "Thanks."

Normally, I would slink off to the juniors' section, but with Elyse here I feel emboldened to stay put. *This is America, lady.* She gives us a tight smile and retreats.

"You like hanging out with him, right?" says Elyse.

"Yeah," I say. "I do."

"It would just be more of that," says Elyse.

"But what would we *do*?"

Elyse laughs. "I don't know . . . talk, watch movies, make out, go out to eat. Normal stuff. What do you think couples do?"

I think about this, and I realize I never got this far, even in my daydreams.

"My imagination kind of goes blank after he asks me to be his girlfriend," I say.

"Either you want to find out what happens next or you don't," says Elyse. She makes it sound so easy.

———

So here I am, in his car, doing what I couldn't put off any longer: talking to the boy I've liked since I was twelve. My first kiss.

It takes Mitch a while to launch into it. He pretends there is no "it," actually, and talks about all the normal things. He asks me about my weekend, and I tell him I quit student council. When he asks me why, I say it was boring, which is true but incomplete. Ingrid has texted me like eighteen times begging me to change my mind, but I don't feel like getting into that. Boys don't really understand the nuances of girl-to-girl social dynamics. Or at least Mitch doesn't. One time I complained about Cara and Audrey's closeness, and he suggested I try getting to know Audrey better. (*???*)

After a while it starts to seem like he'll never get to the point, and I grow irritable, responding more and more curtly to everything he says until I'm grunting half syllables just to prove I'm listening. I can't live like this. I'm crawling out of my skin waiting for it. I think of Elyse going straight for her pretzel, and I take a breath and make myself say it.

"What did you want to talk about, really?" I say.

He was talking about music, I realize suddenly. I have cut him off. "Sorry," I add.

He glances at me on the way to looking over his shoulder, and drifts into the right-turn lane. We pull into a church parking lot. The sign reads HOLY OAK LUTHERAN: *JESUS LIVES HERE!* A bit arrogant, I think. One thing I like about Catholics: no jokey signs. You're either coming in or you're not.

Mitch parks and stares at the wheel, where his hand is slumped at six o'clock. For as long as I live I will remember my driver's ed instructor teaching us why the correct steering position is hands at ten o'clock and two o'clock, or, if you must, nine and three—it has to do with where your arms fly when the airbag explodes from the wheel. A man driving with his hands slung at six could very well end up punching himself in the balls. I feel I should warn Mitch, but the timing isn't right.

"I like you," he says. "A lot."

It's everything I've waited years and years to hear. Mitch was the ideal, but any boy might have done, at some point, just to know it was possible. I'd started to doubt that. I thought once I heard it, it would settle something in me for good. I would have proof I was likable, and I would feel at peace. I thought I would feel like a woman. A person in a body and not just this agonizing, free-floating brain.

I also imagined I'd know what to say back. But I don't.

"Are you going to say anything?" asks Mitch.

Wouldn't we both like to know. His voice shakes just a little, and this breaks my heart.

"Yes," I say. "I mean, I don't know. Obviously, I like you. I like hanging out with you."

He smiles, then stops. "Wait. I can't tell if you meant that the way I meant it."

Now I am sure I'm going to cry.

"I don't know if I do, either," I say quietly.

I feel him watching me. "Will you look at me?" he says, so I do.

He leans in ever so slightly, and I lean back. It is instantaneous, a reflex I didn't see coming and couldn't stop. I hate myself for it. His whole face drops.

"I don't get it," he says. "We hang out all the time. You text me. *You* kissed *me*."

"I know," I say.

"Well, what are you feeling? Maybe I can help," he says.

I doubt this very much. I start a dozen sentences in my head, but they all sound wrong. My throat feels like it might close up for good.

"Okay, fine," says Mitch. He puts the car in gear and pulls out of the lot. Somehow I manage to hold back the tears until I'm at my front door and he's driving away.

I text Cara to invite myself over. She's reluctant until I tell her I need to talk about Mitch. When I get to her house, I see Audrey's car parked in the driveway. *Great.*

I ring the doorbell and wait for what feels like ten minutes before Cara's brother opens the door.

"Hi, Abram," I say.

He grunts and makes his way back down to the basement. Audrey and Cara are in the living room. Four cans of lime sparkling water sit on the coffee table alongside a half-eaten package of Red Vines. Audrey is reclined on the couch, with Cara cross-legged on the floor. Cara will always choose the floor over any seat of any kind. It's pathological.

"Hey," we all say.

I go to the mini-fridge and help myself to a lime water. I press the cold can to my left cheek and then my right.

"What happened?" says Cara.

I sit down next to her, take a Red Vine from the bag. "Um," I say, hoping they don't hear that I've been crying and could cry again any moment. "He told me he likes me."

Audrey yelps.

"That's a good thing, right?" asks Cara.

"I didn't say anything back," I explain.

"Literally not *anything*?"

So I explain it, pausing to clarify when Cara or Audrey has a follow-up question. They have trouble understanding how we got from me telling him I like him, too, to me being dropped off to cry on my front steps. *Join the club.*

"You're probably just overwhelmed because this is the first time this has happened to you," says Cara.

"Aw," says Audrey.

I consider murdering them both. But maybe they're right.

"Did this happen to you the first time?" I ask them.

"Not really," says Audrey.

"Well, kind of, if you count Nate," says Cara. Nate was Cara's sixth-grade boyfriend, whom she famously threw up on at the spring dance, before we were friends. Not *on,* she insists— *near.* But really, when it comes to vomit, "near" is "on."

Nate counts to me because I need someone to count. Because I often feel that I am five years behind everyone else my age, which lines up just about right. Finally, at sixteen, I am eleven.

"Can we watch TV?" I say. "I don't want to think about this anymore."

So Cara puts on a cooking show, and I keep thinking about it anyway. Of course I do.

———

Tonight at work, an hour into my shift, Justin comes over to tell Kristy and me that it's slow and one of us can go home. He doesn't care who: *Just decide amongst yourselves,* he says. Kristy and I look at each other. We both know it's her. She unties her apron, practically jogging off the floor. The next four hours stretch in front of me like open desert. The notion that I have ever before survived a shift at La Baguette now sounds implausible at best. I wish Elyse were here. I almost hate that we've become friends, because working here without her is agonizing, and it wasn't like that before she started. It was bad, of course, but not *as* bad.

I take my meal break at seven-thirty, using my fifty percent discount to get my half 'n' half for $4.50 (plus tax) instead of $8.99 (plus tax). I get the same thing I always do: chicken-and-wild-rice soup, a chicken Caesar salad, and a giant Diet Pepsi I'll drink all of but hate for not being Diet Coke. People are obsessed with our chicken-and-wild-rice soup in a way I think they would not be if they saw the giant plastic vats it arrives in. This food tastes good to me only in the context of its convenience and cheapness, and I have long known that as soon as I stop working here, I will never eat here again.

"Mary," I hear Justin say.

I look over, and he taps the watch on his wrist. I look around the restaurant, to the exactly four customers quietly eating their sandwiches and soups, to the nobody in line. I watch Justin watch me take another slow, *slowww* bite of salad. His rodent eyes narrow.

"Wrap it up," he adds. He is furious but largely impotent, shocked every time one of his young female subordinates doesn't collapse under the weight of his authority. I wonder what his life is like outside La Baguette. I picture him in pajamas, brushing his teeth, and feel a weird mix of disgust and tenderness toward him. I always feel sorry for any man I think too much about.

I finish my soup and salad and take a big gulp of Diet Pepsi before refilling it at the fountain. When I get back to the register, it's 7:51. I sneak my phone from my back pocket: no texts. No anything. Mitch hasn't spoken to me since dropping me off three days ago. Cara hasn't asked for an update since I went to her house that night. I've texted Elyse twice since we went to the mall, and although she replied, she hasn't texted me first in a week. For a truly desperate moment I consider telling Dax what I'm dealing with, but thankfully embarrassment wins out. I say nothing. I press play on my mental recording of that day in the car with Mitch, trying to find the moment where I went wrong.

The next day I'm telling Kelly about Justin, and she starts to laugh, hard, beyond what I would have thought counselors were allowed to do.

"You're funny," she says.

A bloom of happiness opens in my chest. Nobody has ever said this to me before. *I* thought I was funny, but at a certain point that kind of claim requires evidence.

Kelly also tells me that I don't have to kiss Mitch again, and I don't have to make him my boyfriend. I tell her I know these things, and she tells me she knows I know but thinks it's important to give girls permission to say no.

"I want to want to say yes," I counter.

"Is that the same thing?" she says.

I don't answer, but I know she knows that I know it's not.

The time has come: finals week, the last before winter break.

In English, where the final is a group project on one of eight books assigned to us, I do my part, because I don't think it's fair to bring down my teammates just because I'm determined to not try. Historically, I've taken the lead in group projects, as someone always must, and I can tell everyone expects it. Luckily for us, my group also includes Mariah Ross, who is very smart and very serious about literature. Once there might have been a power struggle between us, but now I am happy to do exactly what she asks of me and no more.

Elsewhere, I am free to live and die by my own efforts. I have four exams, one paper, one freebie in the form of art class.

I find it invigorating to walk among my harried, nervous peers, not caring. This time last year I was flipping through Spanish vocab note cards at lunch, thoroughly embarrassing Cara, but this year I sit calmly, eating my sandwich and thinking about other things, like Mitch and sex and work and Elyse and death and Christmas and what if I dyed my hair black. I think I am the wrong kind of pale.

At lunch Cara and Audrey and I talk only about what we will do over winter break, and for this I am grateful. Audrey is going to her family's cabin up north. Cara is going up to join them for a few days. They are sheepish about this, but I don't care (much). I will be working as much as possible, reading for fun, watching every *Star Wars* movie ever made with Peter. I don't tell them this part. Cara asks me if I will see Mitch, and I tell her I don't know. "Hopefully," I add, and this satisfies her enough to move on.

I wake up the first morning of winter break to find a notification that my report card is ready to be viewed.

The damage is as follows:

> Calculus: C-
> Physics: C-
> English: B-
> History: C-
> Spanish: B-
> Art: A-

There is something I hate about all those minuses lined up, one after another. It would have helped, I think, to have one solid, middle-of-the-road letter there, even if it was a C . . . *especially* if it was a C. But then I remind myself this was the point. Or it's the natural result of the point. I stopped trying, mostly. And now here I am.

I got over the guilt at seeing anything below an A- months ago, but I guess I'd hoped that by the time I got to this part I'd know better what I was doing, and why. I'd pictured transcribing my report card into my journal, and drawing a series of meaningful conclusions. But I don't like looking at it, and I don't feel like writing it down. It isn't interesting. It's average.

I present my grades to my parents at dinner, because a paper copy will come in the mail anyway and I'd just as soon get it over with and move on.

My mom is angry, fixated on the B⁻ in both English and Spanish, even though there is worse.

"Spanish is easy for you. You love English," she says. I've never said either of these things, but I guess I must have made them obvious. "I don't understand how you managed this." She holds my phone, studying it like a Magic Eye that might reveal a secret message: *Your daughter is performing below her ability on purpose. CALL THE POLICE.* She can't look at it anymore. She hands the phone to my dad. He glances at it, then sets it down next to me. He folds his hands in a fist that hides his mouth. I've seen this routine play out for my brother's benefit dozens of times: angry mom, quietly disappointed dad. She warms them up, he knocks them flat. I have often thought they should do prisons.

He takes so long to think that the silence starts to scream. Even Mom looks annoyed. I glance at Peter, who chews his pork chop happily, entirely in his own world. This is the greatest gift I have ever given him. *Merry Christmas, Peter.*

"Is this all because of a boy?" says my dad.

Oh, I think. I was not prepared for this. My chest burns. I'm indignant, but not as much as I am embarrassed.

"No," I sputter. Then, immediately, I'm unsure. Wasn't it, a little bit, because of a boy? But no.

"No," I say again.

"You can tell us if you have a boyfriend," says my mom.

"He's not my boyfriend," I say. Then it occurs to me: the perfect escape. "We broke up." I try to look sad. It's easy. I *am* sad.

My parents exchange looks. My mom softens. My dad sighs. *Bingo,* I think.

I look at Peter. *Liar,* he thinks.

"Okay," says my dad. "You and Mom can talk about that later."

I nod, sadly, and stand up to clear my plate, hoping that if I treat the conversation as done now, it will be. But when I risk a glance, my dad is watching my attempted escape in disbelief, his palms held open in a gesture that reminds me of Jesus Christ.

"You're grounded, obviously," he says.

I drop my plate in the dishwasher hard enough to make needless noise, soft enough for plausible deniability. I cross my arms over my chest, overcome with disgust for myself. *Not again.* "What are the terms?" I say. "I don't even do anything."

"That's true," says Peter.

My dad shoots him a warning look.

"No friends for two weeks," says my dad. "Phone goes in the Velcro thing overnight." He is, of course, making this up on the spot, and it's the arbitrariness that bothers me most. However, I know from having watched Peter that protest will only make it worse. If I accept it now, there's a decent chance he'll forget his own timeline halfway into it.

"My phone's my alarm," I say, knowing full well it's not a strong argument. I hear his response before he says it.

"So's an alarm clock," he says. "You can borrow mine."

———

I picked up shifts almost every day over break except Christmas Day and New Year's Day, when La Baguette is closed. At the time it seemed smart—I would make *so much money*—but when I wake up to work the first of thirteen shifts over sixteen days, I'm not so sure. How much will I make, anyway? I do the math before I get out of bed: eighty-two hours at ten dollars an hour equals $820. Maybe $600 after taxes. Two-thirds of that goes a pathetically short distance toward funding the hypothetical college I haven't yet chosen and can't stand thinking about, leaving me with $200. Minus $50 to fill up the tank with gas and another $50 to pay my mom back for money I borrowed to buy Christmas presents for her and my dad and Peter. Grand total kept: 100 big ones.

It's $100 more than I'd have if I didn't work the thirteen shifts. I know this, but I'm still mad. I once heard that AJ Pratt gets $500 a month from her parents *just for clothing*. Like, $500 per month *above and beyond* whatever her allowance is. This is the most repellent piece of gossip I have ever digested, and I'm so jealous I could cry.

I should get a job with tips, I think, like a server at a sit-down restaurant. But no. I can barely stand the customers at La Baguette, and I have to interact with them only once.

The crowd at La Baguette on a weekday is different from what I'm used to. It's primarily moms alone, or moms with babies, or moms with babies plus their mom friends with their babies. The second-best mall in the area is nearby, and they come here in droves between stopping there and at Target, or vice versa, doing a fifth or sixth round of Christmas shopping. In celebration of the season, we have sugar cookies frosted like snowmen and reindeer, which look better than they taste.

We also have two seasonal soups: winter squash and turkey chili, the latter of which Kristy says gave her diarrhea. She is sexually confident enough to say that kind of thing in front of boys. I can't understand it.

My shift starts at ten, and I spend most of the first two hours ringing up early lunches and clearing dishes and checking the clock over and over, because Elyse's shift starts at noon. Finally, at 12:02, she walks in, sees me, and grins.

"You're late," announces Justin as she reaches the registers.

"I had to stop for tampons," she says, a little loudly.

He shakes his head and moves on to the food line. Elyse winks at me: a dork move she makes unprecedentedly cool. I want to be her.

Elyse goes into the back and returns a minute later in her apron, visor, and name tag. She logs in to the register next to me just in time for a rush of customers. For thirty minutes, it's just, *Hi, what can I get you? What size? Anything else? Here's your buzzer.* Then the buzzer system goes down, which it tends to do twice a day, and we start telling the customers that we'll call their names instead. Mostly they accept the new procedure without question, but then I get a lady who can't believe this is happening to her.

"So I have to stand by the counter till you call me?" she says.

"Yes," I say. "I mean, you don't have to be *right* here."

"But if I want to be able to hear it . . . ," she says.

"Within earshot would be good, yeah." Over her shoulder I watch the line grow ever longer.

"All the tables are going to fill up," she says.

What I *should* do, per customer-first training, is offer to bring her food to her table directly. What I actually do is shrug. "Good luck," I say.

She huffs angrily and takes about a hundred years to drop the change I've handed her into one of those ugly little beaded coin purses she pulls from the depths of her plum Longchamp tote. Behind her another woman watches, plainly disgusted. I think, *Thank God, an ally,* but then she's crabby with me, too, especially after I tell her we don't have black bean soup today.

"Why not?" she demands.

"We don't serve black bean soup on Tuesdays or Thursdays," I reply, gesturing to the alternating soup menu on the wall behind me.

"I got it last Thursday," she says.

Get a life, I think. "I don't think so," I say.

She blinks at me. "I have yoga on Thursdays. I remember because I came after yoga."

"I don't know what to tell you, but we don't have any unfrozen black bean soup at this time," I say.

The woman grimaces. Nobody who comes to La Baguette wants to know where their soup is coming from. They want to think a middle-aged French lady is making it in the back.

I feel Elyse's foot tap twice against mine in solidarity. I bite the insides of my cheeks to keep from laughing.

"The turkey chili is good," Elyse offers.

The yoga lady looks from me to her and back to me. "Fine," she says. She snatches her receipt from my hand like I stole it from her first. The moment her back is turned, Elyse turns to me and mouths: *Cunt.*

I want to be her *so* bad.

—————

On Christmas morning I wake up at 5:35 and tiptoe across the hall to Peter's room. The light from his desk lamp shines under the door, so I know it's safe to open without knocking. I find him sitting on the floor, sleepily pulling the Connect Four grid from the box he keeps under the bed, unused 364 days of the year. Somehow this has become our only private tradition. When we were young enough to need the rule, Mom set six-thirty as the earliest we could go downstairs to see our presents. Adrenaline or habit still wakes us up early, so now we meet to kill the time.

I take a seat next to Peter and fold my legs under me. I am wearing an XL T-shirt with the Grinch on it that our mom bought me when I was twelve. Peter is wearing his own themed T-shirt featuring Ralphie from *A Christmas Story.* Both shirts are wrinkled from spending all year smooshed at the bottom of our respective dressers. If we don't wear them this morning, Mom will ask us where they are and make us go get them for a family photo. Putting them on the night before saves us all a lot of trouble.

"Red or black?" asks Peter.

I am always red. "Black," I say. I also always lose. Maybe the color has been the problem.

We flip a quarter to see who goes first, and I guess right, so I drop a black disk in the grid near the middle. I love the thick plastic click it makes, and later rows are even better, when the disks clack against each other. It is not the quietest game to have chosen for predawn, as our dad has pointed out.

Of all the open spaces available, Peter drops a red disk on top of mine. Already he is up to something. *Maybe I can distract him if I talk,* I think.

"What are you most hoping you get?" I say, dropping a black disk next to my first one.

Peter names a video game sequel without taking his eyes off the board, dropping a red disk on the bottom row to neighbor mine. As usual, I have no idea what he's going for. I drop my next piece alongside the first two, making three in a row. I know Peter will cut me off on his next turn. But what else am I supposed to do?

"I hate this game," I say.

"You're pretty bad at it," says Peter.

"It's for kids," I say.

"And yet . . ." Peter's disk drops next to my little row: *thunk.* "What did you ask for?"

I picture the list hanging on the bulletin board in the home office. I made it in August, which feels like years ago now. This is standard for me: drafting a list of desired items the second the school year starts and then revising it as necessary over the next few months. But this year I haven't touched it since that first draft. I feel pleased with myself, realizing this.

"Books, mostly," I say. "Clothes, bath stuff."

Peter nods. I look at the grid and realize he is about to win unless I stop him, so I do. He is annoyingly unsurprised, and I realize he only *wanted* me to think he was about to win.

"Isn't it weird that every year we write a list of things we want and give it to our parents and then one day they give some of those things to us?" says Peter.

"It is weird," I say. "But remember the no-list year?"

Peter grimaces. "All the time."

When I was twelve and Peter was ten, our parents—well, our mom—came to a similar conclusion: that Christmas lists were mercenary, impersonal, and rude, actually. So she abolished them, and we all shopped blind. It was a disaster. Everyone but my dad cried, and even he had two Bloody Marys before noon.

"Well, what did you get me?" says Peter. He still hasn't taken his eyes off the board. It's half-full now. The clicks get quieter and quieter the closer we get to the top.

"I'm not telling you that," I say. (I bought him two paperbacks, one from his list and one I picked out myself. I will be devastated if he doesn't read it. This holiday creates so much potential for hurt feelings.)

"Connect four," Peter says, boredly.

"God damn it," I say. We check the clock (5:48) and start again.

———

After we open presents and scoop up all the wrapping paper and put our presents back under the tree in neat piles, and my parents pour themselves more coffee and Peter and I finally brush our teeth, it's 7:12, and I have the whole day to think about Mitch. I finally dreamt about him last night, though the details are hazy and his face wasn't quite his. But I knew it was him. We were at a party in a house with two pools, and all I wanted was for him to kiss me in front of people so they'd know and I'd know his love for me was real. And he did. As a movie plot it was saccharine, heavy-handed. As an image playing and replaying in my mind, it was compelling. Each time we kissed, my heart soared. Then it went away. So

I replayed it to feel myself stir, over and over, a little weaker each time. Why did I feel this way when I imagined kissing him and not when I actually kissed him? All the imagery was the same: his handsome face, strong hands pulling me closer, soft lips. Maybe it would have worked if I'd only had the nerve to try again. I'd been warned by plenty of articles found online late at night that no first kiss is perfect, but apparently I'd expected it anyway.

My mom thinks my mood means I hated my presents, so I assure her I do not.

"What is it, then?" she says. She sits on the footstool of the armchair where I'm folded up, trying and failing to read one of my new books. I don't normally talk to my mother about boys, except to acknowledge that some are cute, but the only alternative I can think of is to say I'm mulling over my poor academic performance this past semester, and that seems worse.

"I just feel a little sad about Mitch," I say.

My mom's shoulders relax instantly. "I'm sorry," she says. "Holidays are especially hard."

"Yeah," I say. "I guess."

"Did it just not work out?" she says.

"Yeah," I say. "I don't know." *I'm saying nothing.* Does she realize that?

"Well, I'm here, if you want to talk about it," she says, but isn't that what we're doing right now? I say okay, and turn to my book, and she pats my knee and leaves the room. I'm sorry the conversation is over, even though I don't know what else I could have said even if I'd wanted to say more. I wish she'd read my mind so I didn't have to say any of it. Maybe my thoughts would make more sense in someone else's head.

———

The day after Christmas is a wasteland at La Baguette. Anyone with money is taking the day off, still clinging to the holiday at home. Nobody is in the mood for a bread bowl. Soup might sound good in theory, given that it's minus three degrees outside (minus eighteen if you count the windchill, and you have to count the windchill), but it's just cold enough that nobody wants to travel for it. They will make Campbell's instead or order wonton soup for delivery. I get in the car and turn it on twenty minutes before I have to leave, just to give it enough time to melt the frost on my windows.

Still, I have looked forward to this day, because I knew it'd be dead, and because Elyse is working, too. Besides the bagel maker, who is just leaving when we arrive, we are the first ones in the parking lot, no manager in sight. We rush through the doors, shivering and stamping our boots on the mud mat. Elyse drops her bag on the counter and looks around. For now, the restaurant is lawless and ours. It smells overwhelmingly of cinnamon crunch bagel.

"Who is it, Jerry? Or Justin?" she asks.

I push through the swinging door to the back and trace my finger over the schedule. "Jerry," I say.

"Really?" says Elyse. "He's never late."

"I know," I say. I wonder if he's in a ditch, like me that one time. I wonder, briefly, if he's dead.

Then I feel terrible, so I add, "I hope he's okay."

Elyse gives me a look. "Uh, I'm sure he's fine."

And sure enough, Jerry walks in two minutes later. He doesn't apologize or acknowledge his lateness, because that would mean letting us know he knows he did something that we'd get in trouble for. He just gives us a curt nod and runs his hand over his shellacked hair helmet and disappears quickly into the office.

Elyse and I start prepping the restaurant to open: I pull bagels from the cooling racks and put them in bins, then clip on the labels: cinnamon crunch, poppy seed, blueberry, everything, onion, garlic, pumpkin, plain. Elyse arranges the cookies and pastries and puts their corresponding labels in upright metal stems. When I first started, we used these as table number stands, too. Jerry and co. were experimenting with table service then, but it cost too much money to have an extra person on each shift to run meals out to tables, and then customers felt pressured to tip, which made them angry. So we stopped, modeling the new system after the DMV.

As we prepare and clean, Elyse and I ask each other about our Christmases, which sound very different. Elyse's older brother and his girlfriend and their cousins and aunts and uncles came over to play "White Elephant" and make sugar candy and drink soju, a Korean spirit that Elyse compares to sweet vodka.

"Your parents let you drink?" I say.

Elyse laughs. "Just a couple, Officer," she says, and I blush. "It's a special occasion."

She continues her story, about some inside family joke involving a whoopee cushion passed around every year, but I'm distracted by my imagined picture of Elyse's raucous family Christmas.

"Isn't that funny?" says Elyse.

"Yes," I say, not laughing.

"You're not listening," she says.

"I'm sorry," I say. "Just repeat the last part."

"Too late," she says. "You stepped on my joke. It's behind us."

"I'm sorry!" I laugh. "Forgive me!" I grab her by the shoulders and shake her a little, pleading. My hands feel prickly where they touch her, and I have to make myself let go.

Elyse looks at me funny, but I tell myself there's no way she could have seen it on my face when I don't even know what "it" is. But there is an "it," I think, and this worries me.

"What are we missing?" she says. She exhales forcefully and surveys the dining room. A once-white dishrag hangs limply from the fist propped against her hip. For the thousandth time since I started working here, I wonder when, if ever, those rags were last replaced. I scan the laminated opening checklist on the counter.

"Coffee," I say. "I think that's it."

Elyse nods and turns from me to start the brewing machine. I have the briefest—probably paranoid—sensation that she's mad at me. But then she starts up again about Christmas, chattering happily as she supervises the machine while it fills one pot and then another with oily black coffee. And I listen. I really do try to listen. But mostly I wonder what just happened, if anything happened at all.

That night, long after I've gotten home and torn off my polo and washed the soup smell out of my hair, I text Elyse to say *I'm sorry if—* No, *I'm sorry that I was weird earlier.* I don't know if this is the right word for it, but I don't know how else to bring it up except to apologize, broadly, for who I am.

When? she replies.

You weren't, she adds.

OK, I text. *I thought maybe I upset you.*

You def didn't, she writes.

I don't like that "def." That "def" makes me feel like she knows exactly what I mean but won't say so.

Well, great, I reply. *I apologize for apologizing. So sorry.*

Hahaha, she texts. I smile, overcome by a whoosh of relief. It always feels like a risk to text someone a joke without adding an "lol," and so much more satisfying when they understand your meaning without it.

I wait a minute to see if she'll text again. It feels important to know she wants to text me and isn't just responding to my nudging. I just want her to like me. I want her to text me even when she has nothing to say, like real friends do.

I wait long enough that my screen goes dark. When it lights up again, it's not Elyse but Mitch. Calling me.

I don't know what to do, so I wait for the ringing to stop and his name to disappear from my screen, and then I text Elyse—*omg Mitch just called me*—without thinking about how, maybe, I should've saved that particular message for Cara instead.

Just now? she replies.

Yeah.

Did you answer?

No.

???

These question marks sum up so much of my life right now, I think.

Idk, I respond. I'm not sure what else there is to say.

Yeah.

I'm boring her. I'm boring myself.

Sorry, I text. *Sidetracked.*

She sends sideways emoji eyes—I apologized again.

I know, I know, but I am, I write. *Idk what's going on with me.*

Are you gonna call him back?

It feels like this question means more than it says. But maybe I'm just losing my mind.

I guess I should, I say.

Yeah, she writes. *Good luck.*

Thanks.

I've wilted in bed as we continued texting, so I sit up straighter and try to prepare myself to call Mitch back. I try to remember how it felt to be excited to talk to him, but all that does is make me wonder what changed, and what's wrong with me that something did. Because obviously it's me and not him. He has been consistent, patient, sweet, and clear. I am used to blaming all my ill-fated crushes on the boy, for failing to notice me, or flirting with me without meaning it, or revealing himself to be a jerk by daring to date someone else. It's a familiar kind of pain to dispense with boys this way, before I really know them. But I know Mitch. He is not a jerk. He did nothing wrong. So I take a breath and press my thumb to his name on my screen.

He picks up after two rings.

"Hi," he says.

"Hey," I say. "Sorry I missed your call."

"It's okay. I was kind of relieved when you didn't pick up."

I can't help it; I laugh. "I know the feeling."

"Yeah. So."

"So."

"Yeah, so, do you want to go for a drive tomorrow or something?" he says in a rush. "It doesn't have to be—I know you don't—it's just, I miss you. I miss hanging out with you."

My heart breaks into a thousand little pieces. It actually, physically hurts me, how good he is, how perfect this should have been.

"I miss hanging out with you, too," I say. And I mean it. "I just can't—"

"I know," he says. "I get it. Well—I don't actually get it completely, but I accept it." I wonder if he can hear my mouth stretch into a smile. "So I'm wondering if we can be friends."

"Okay," I say. "Yeah. I'd like that."

"So tomorrow?"

"I work at two," I say. "But I could do morning." As of today, I've cleared eleven, maybe twelve, days of my grounding, which I'm pretty sure is close enough.

"You're killing me," says Mitch. I know most non-school nights he's up till two or three in the morning, listening to music, playing video games. Whatever it is boys do in their alone time. "Okay. I can pick you up at . . . ten."

"Sounds good," I say. "See you then."

"Bye, Mary," he says, and hangs up before I can say bye back.

I think about texting Elyse to tell her what just happened but quickly decide not to. I'm not really sure she'd care, and I feel defensive at the thought of having to explain myself. Maybe I've reached the self-assuredness stage, when I no longer need or seek external approval of my actions. The thought makes me laugh out loud. *Good one, Mary.*

When I tell my mom that Mitch is picking me up to go for a drive, she freezes where she sits on the floor, reorganizing our family's extensive collection of Tupperware.

"It's not like that," I say quickly. But even I don't know what I mean. "He just wants to be friends now. I mean, so do I."

"Are you sure?" my mom says.

I search her face for hopefulness to resent, but there is none. It is possible she just wants me to be okay, boyfriend or no boyfriend.

"Pretty sure," I say. How can I be fully sure I want something I've never had? This, at least, is Cara's argument. The other week she made the comparison to brussels sprouts: sure, as a kid, she thought they were disgusting. But years later, they came as a side at a restaurant, roasted in salt and pepper and olive oil, and she loved them. I knew what she was going for, so I let it go. But I wondered then, and I wonder still: *What is the equivalent of salting and roasting a boy?*

"Well, just be honest with him," my mom says. She's resumed stacking, and I'm soothed by the sound of each rubbery plastic vessel nesting inside the next. "And with yourself," she adds.

She is not looking at me now, which is fortunate, because my eyes well up before I can stop them. PMS, I think.

———

Mitch arrives in my driveway at 10:08, and I scramble to the door to put on my shoes and yell that I'm leaving, worried that if I take too long, my mom will insist on inviting him in to meet the parents. Fortunately, my dad is back at work, and maybe it's his absence that saves me.

"Have fun!" yells my mom from the kitchen. "Lock the door behind you!"

"I know!" I yell back. "Bye!"

I slip out, lock the door, and wave at Mitch through the windshield. He smiles sleepily.

"Did you just wake up?" I ask as I slide in next to him.

"Maybe," he says. "Can we get coffee?"

"Yes, please," I say, though I don't drink it. Mitch reverses down my driveway, and I study him in quick sidelong glances. His hair, normally aloft, is flat, giving him childlike bangs I find upsetting. The conditions for my attraction to him are so specific. I often wonder what other girls feel when their boyfriends have bad hair days or wear bad jeans. I suppose I can believe they don't mind, but I cannot believe they don't notice.

"How was your Christmas?" I ask.

Mitch laughs. "Fine," he says. "My mom's boyfriend gave me a pellet gun without telling her, so that was a whole thing."

"So, literally *A Christmas Story*," I say.

He shakes his head, blank.

"The movie? 'You'll shoot your eye out'?"

"Maybe I've heard that," he says.

"Anyway," I say. "Congrats on your gun."

"It *is* pretty cool," he says. "I thought he hated me, but then he wanted to do target practice on some Coke cans."

"That's good, then," I say.

Mitch flips on his left blinker just where I feared he would, directing us toward the only Starbucks within ten miles.

"Can we do the drive-through?" I ask.

"How come?"

"It's just easier," I say. He gives me a look, and I sigh. "AJ and them are always in there." Located on the border between my middle-class suburb and the gated community, the Starbucks provides a neutral meetup spot for the rich popular kids and the middle-class popular kids to get together and discuss their shared disdain for the rest of us. They are there every Saturday, and most mornings over winter break, rehashing the night prior, plotting the night ahead.

"So?" says Mitch.

He looks at me. I look at him. I remember the old rumor that Mitch was the popular kids' pot dealer. They like him. Or at least they respect him. Fear him, maybe.

"Okay," I say. "Yeah, we can go in."

Mitch parks at a respectable distance, and I wipe my palms on my jeans, zip my coat up to my eyebrows, and exit the car. It's cold, frigid enough that my nose hairs freeze together in the seven seconds it takes to cross the parking lot. Mitch holds open the door for me, and I groan into the collar of my jacket. I wanted him to go in first, as my shield.

Once inside I glance to my right, and sure enough, there they are, spread over the one pleather couch and two armchairs like it's their own living room. Like all the chain restaurants inside the fancy neighborhood, this Starbucks has been made over to mimic a fussy, underused parlor that just happens to sell fast food.

I speed to the counter without looking. I know I saw AJ and Caroline, Keely and her boyfriend, Tyler, Jonah (AJ's boyfriend), and Naomi, but their presence felt bigger than six people. I order a peppermint mocha because it seems most likely to not taste like coffee and turn to ask Mitch what he wants, but he's not there. He is in the fake living room, saying hello to his clients.

I pay for my drink and try not to fume. I expected that he would talk to them, obviously. Would it have been nice if he'd waited until after he bought his coffee with me, seeing as I don't even drink coffee, so that we could approach them together? Sure. Yes. Would it have been nice if I'd wanted to be his girlfriend, like he asked? Well . . . Also yes.

"Actually, can I also get a tall black coffee, too?" I say, scooting back to the register.

I wait for his order and then carry them both over, shaking with nerves and grumbling in my head. I have to tap Mitch on the back with my elbow for him to finally turn to me.

"Here," I say, and as I hand him his coffee, I take another look at what I'm dealing with. Everyone I registered before is here, plus Missy, whom I missed because she's sitting on the floor. I think of La Baguette's carpeting, and all the things it's seen, and I feel slightly sorry for Missy's ass-kissing ass.

"Oh, hey," says AJ. She looks from me to Mitch and back, putting it together. "What's up?"

"Not much," I say, forgetting, as usual, that this is always, *always* a rhetorical question.

"Anyway," says Caroline. "You should come."

"You too, Mary," says AJ.

Caroline turns sharply to AJ and smiles. I know thinly suppressed rage when I see it. "Caroline is having a party on Friday," AJ adds.

"Cool," I say. "Thanks." Not for a second do I imagine I might actually attend this party, but I recognize that I've been given a favor.

"Shall we?" I ask Mitch, pleading with my eyes.

"Yeah, we're gonna jet," he says.

Jet? But it works for him. I give a dumb little wave, which doesn't, and we leave. The whole excruciating exchange is over within fifteen seconds, and still I know it will keep me up for several nights to come. At Mitch's car I pull on the handle until he finally unlocks it, and I clamber into the quickly fading warmth and safety.

"That was weird," I say. I try a sip of my mocha, which tastes like burnt hot chocolate. But then I take another sip, and it's better. *This is how it happens.*

"Why was it weird?" says Mitch.

"Uh, because those people aren't my friends and clearly don't actually want me at their party?"

"AJ's really nice," he says. "I don't think she would've asked if she didn't mean it."

"If she's *so nice,* then that's exactly what she'd do." Honestly, he can be so simple.

"Well, I'm gonna go," he says. "It'd be cool if you came, too."

I don't have an answer for this, so I let the suggestion sit in the air. He means as friends, I think. I hope. I'm not sure I have it in me to explain myself again.

The light turns green, and Mitch exits onto the highway going south toward the city. I know which route he'll take today because we've done it so many times: across the bridge, exit by the university, drive through the artsy neighborhood around it, then back on the freeway going north toward home. It's as if he needs to check every so often to make sure somewhere cooler than our suburb still exists.

"How do you know them anyway?" I ask.

"AJ and them?"

I nod.

"The people we both go to school with?"

There is something funny about the way he refers to AJ and her friends, a sort of reverence I didn't expect.

"People say you're their dealer," I say.

He shrugs.

"Is that a no, or . . . ?"

He shakes his head and rolls his eyes, and I realize too late that I've offended him.

"I'm sorry," I say. "I don't care either way, I just wondered." This is a lie. I care, but maybe only because I want to know everything.

"I sold a couple of those guys some weed before, yeah," he says.

"Which ones?" I ask.

Mitch shoots me a look.

"Sorry. Doesn't matter."

"You're pretty judgy, Mary Davies," he says. He is smiling, but I can tell he means it, too.

"I'm not judging," I reply. "I just like knowing things."

"So you can judge."

"No," I say. "Maybe." I pause. "It's not like I really, intellectually think pot is even bad, or whatever. It would just be context for that person."

"You should get to know them if what you really want is context," says Mitch.

I watch him bite the skin around his thumbnail, which still has a chip of black polish hanging on for dear life, and I realize something: just like everybody else, Mitch Kulikosky wants the popular kids to like him. There is a desperation to his insistence that they are worth knowing that just doesn't make sense otherwise. This information disappoints me, even as I decide he's right. It's not so much that I think I'm qualified to judge, or that I'm superior, as it is that I need examples of lives against which to measure mine. How does anyone know they're performing a human being correctly without watching other human beings to see what they're doing? I may be incapable of love, but if I knew that, say, Keely and Tyler bought drugs at least once, maybe that would soothe me somehow.

I tell Mitch I'll go to the party if he promises not to abandon me the second we get there.

"Deal," he says. "It'll be fun."

Famous last words.

———

A miracle happens, and it snows all night and all day leading up to Caroline's party. I work the early shift at La Baguette with Kristy, and by the time I'm done there's a foot of snow on the ground, with more coming down fast. I creep home, taking every turn so slowly the car hardly moves forward. The plows are out in full force, but the snow piles up in their wake, glittering and dangerous.

At home I shower and check my phone a thousand times, waiting for a text from Mitch letting me know the party's off. At six, the second I finish dinner, I text him.

Is the party still happening?

Yeah? he replies.

Not snowed out?

Lol, he replies. *Sorry, you still have to come.*

Ugh, I text back, smiling. It's nice to be able to joke around with him like this. I feel so much more comfortable with him now that I'm not worried about *being* with him. I know this makes no sense, but I don't have time to think about that. He's picking me up at eight-thirty, which means I have only two and a half hours to get ready.

No, I think, catching myself. The old Mary might have started doing her hair and makeup ridiculously early and then sat on her hands for hours trying not to sweat through the pits of her party shirt, but no more. I look around my room, hoping to be inspired by some all-encompassing, time-consuming activity, but all I see is my laptop, and I know I can't focus on Netflix right now. I cross the hall and knock on Peter's door.

I expect to find him on his computer or playing video games on his Switch, but instead he's sitting on the floor, staring at a booklet open at his feet. He looks up and then back, silently granting me permission to enter. I pull his comforter over his unmade bed and sit on the end of it. His bed takes five seconds to make, and yet he has never once done it voluntarily. Not that it matters.

Peter remains focused on his pages, unconcerned that I'm here needing to be entertained. "What are you reading?" I say, annoyed.

"Shakespeare," he says.

I laugh. He closes the booklet and holds it up so I can read the title: *A Midsummer Night's Dream.*

Oh. "Why're you reading that?"

"I'm not reading, I'm memorizing," he says. "Spring play."

Once he says it, I remember seeing a couple of flyers around school before break. I've been to just one school play, as a freshman: also Shakespeare, *Twelfth Night.* It was pretty good.

Our drama teacher is very well liked and apparently more talented than one might expect a Midwestern suburban high school drama teacher to be.

"You're gonna try out?"

"You don't have to sound so skeptical," says Peter.

"Sorry," I say. "I just mean, I had no idea you were even interested."

He shrugs. "It seems fun. Freshmen don't get cast very often, though."

"I suppose not," I say. "But it's really cool you're gonna try." My chest swells with affection for him. He is so gangly and vulnerable there on the floor. I'd hug him, but I know he'd hate it. "Can you show me a little bit?"

"Like, perform it now?"

"Yeah," I say. "I can read the other part, if you need me to. Who are you auditioning for?"

"Bottom," he says, smiling slightly. "I'll do a monologue." He hands me the booklet and points to where he'll start.

"Great," I say. "Okay, go."

He stands up, closes his eyes, and reopens them completely transformed. He is already nearly six feet tall, but suddenly he's impish and light on his feet. He recites:

"When my cue comes, call me, and I will answer. My next is 'Most fair Pyramus.' Heigh-ho! Peter Quince! Flute the bellows-mender! Snout the tinker! Starveling! God's my life, stol'n hence, and left me asleep! I have had a most rare vision. I have had a dream past the wit of man to say what dream it was. Man is but an ass if he go about to expound this dream. Methought I was— there is no man can say—"

"It's 'tell.'" I say. "'No man can *tell* what . . .'"

His shoulders droop, and I know I've made a mistake. "Keep going," I say, and he finishes strong. I leap off his bed and clap until he swats my hands to stop them.

"You were amazing!" I say.

"Next time lead with that," he says. He is still pleased, I know, but suddenly I feel like crying. I can't, though, or I'll be all puffy at the party.

"Thank you," he adds, recognizing our shared cheek-biting tactic.

"You're *really* good," I say. "I'm really impressed."

"Thanks," he says again. "I'm still working on it."

"When are auditions?"

"January twentieth."

"If you want help practicing before that, just ask me, okay?"

"I'm all right," he says. He doesn't think I mean it.

"No, seriously. I don't do homework anymore. I have a lot more time now."

He stares at me a moment. "You're doing that on purpose?"

"Sort of," I say.

I hesitate. I don't really want to talk about this, is the thing. Not when I already feel raw. "Not really," I add. "I was kidding."

"Okay," says Peter. He doesn't dig for more information, and for that, too, I love him. "Well, yeah, I'll let you know."

"I can't wait to see you in the play," I say.

"All right—that's enough," he says, and shoos me from his room.

––––––

Mitch is in my driveway at 8:28, which I know because I start watching from my window at 8:20. I rush downstairs before he's parked, replying "Yep" and "I know" to my parents' various reminders about my curfew and driving safely in the snow. They ask again if Caroline's parents will be there and again I say, "Yes, of course." This might even be true, though I don't know for sure—Caroline strikes me as the kind of girl whose parents would buy her beer themselves if it meant she'd be nice to them for even a day. I yell a final goodbye and lock the door behind me, trudging through nearly knee-deep snow to get to Mitch's car. Before leaving I'd had to decide between snow boots for practicality or sneakers for style, and it's immediately clear that I chose wrong.

"You're early," I say when I open the door.

"I was bored," says Mitch. But he's excited, too. I can feel it. His hair is freshly hot-pink and styled, and I'm pretty sure I smell cologne. It's nice—not too much, like some classmates I could name. I think about telling him he smells good and then worry he'll get the wrong idea. I had also worried he'd notice my own attempts at beauty and say something about it, but he doesn't. What a relief.

I notice Mitch has Maps open on his phone and ask if he's ever been to Caroline's before. He shakes his head. "Nah. I've been to a few parties of theirs, but they were always at Tyler's."

"Were they fun?" I ask.

"I don't remember," he smirks.

A pit forms in my stomach. It must also show up on my face, because he elbows me gently in the arm. "Relax," he says. "You don't have to do anything you don't want to do."

"Thanks, Dad," I say, buckling my seat belt, praying it somehow locks me into this seat for the night. I feel both patronized and comforted by his reassurance, his assumption that my first instinct is to not want. But he's right, isn't he? I can't be mad at him for knowing me. Or I shouldn't be.

The rest of the twelve-minute drive is quiet; Mitch doesn't even put on music. He is cautious, braking early at every light, quick to correct course when the wheels spin out slightly on the turn into the gated community. In Caroline's long driveway, after Mitch has parked among the eight or nine other cars here so far, I make him promise to stay by my side, at least at first.

"They're gonna think—" He cuts himself off. "Okay."

I know how the end of that sentence goes. I'm momentarily hurt that this is a mistake he doesn't want other people to make. And then I realize something that delights me.

"You like her," I say.

"What? Who?" says Mitch. His face tints to match his hair. I'm fully grinning now, practically floating out of my seat.

"AJ," I say definitively, though I'm only sixty percent sure. It's something in the way he says her name.

For a moment Mitch looks like he plans to protest, but it falls away fast. "Fine," he says. "Kind of."

I swat him in the chest with my empty glove. "You two-timing son of a bitch."

His eyes widen, incredulous, until the laughter escapes from my throat. "Oh my *God,*" he says, throwing his head back against the seat. He's smiling, though. I feel so good at this moment. I wish this was the party, and there was nobody else to see.

"I did like you, you know," he says. I feel him look at me, and it takes everything I have not to break eye contact for my lap, or the window, or anything else. I feel I owe him this much.

"I know," I say.

"I—" I start again, but I don't know how to finish it. I did like him. I do like him. I might even love him, but not the right way.

"It's okay," says Mitch. "Let's just leave it there."

I nod. I am so grateful, and I am so sorry.

"It's so obvious," he says. "AJ, I mean. I'm no better than Jonah Fucking Lehman."

Jonah Fucking Lehman is AJ's on-again, off-again boyfriend, preordained to date her because of his sculptured face, his family wealth, and his talent for hockey.

"Are they together again?" I ask, trying to remember how they seemed at Starbucks.

Mitch shrugs, as if he doesn't research this question nightly on Instagram.

"Well, it's a good sign she invited you," I say.

"I told you. She's just nice," he says.

I burst into laughter. I can't help it.

Mitch glares at me.

"I'm sorry," I say. "It's just so—"

"Pedestrian."

"I was gonna say 'cute.'" My sweet ex-druggie almost-boyfriend Mitch, in love with the most popular girl in school. "You guys would look great together," I add. "Much more interesting than her and Jonah."

"Fuck off," he says. I can tell what he means is that he loves me, too. Just as friends now, right where we were maybe always meant to be.

Finally there is nothing left to do but go inside. We get out of the car and trudge to the front door. We ring the doorbell and wait. We knock and wait. I press the door handle down, and the door swings open. Immediately, the party's noise floats up to us from below: they're in the basement, from the sounds of it. Mitch and I exchange a look, enter the house, and close the door behind us. There is no turning back now.

The hallway we enter is dark and littered with shoes—mostly snow boots, I note regretfully—so we take ours off quickly and slide on socks along the wood floor. I listen intently for evidence of parental presence, but it's impossible to pick out. The house is huge, and I hope they are in it somewhere, far away, just in case.

Mitch waits for me, seeming to expect me to lead us to the party. "You're kidding," I whisper. He hesitates briefly, almost imperceptibly, but I see these things about him now. He concedes, and directs us through the home's cavernous kitchen to a door left two inches ajar. He thumps down the thickly carpeted stairs, and I follow, holding my breath like I'm expecting toxic fumes. But when we get to the landing, we find only the people we ran into at Starbucks, plus ten or fifteen more, spread across couches and the floor and hovering around a bar in the back. In the middle of the room is a glass coffee table covered with beer cans and a thousand-dollar Bose speaker, playing a song I thought we'd all grown tired of three months ago. It's only a matter of seconds before I find her on the floor, partly obscured by the table and Keely's legs: Hanna. She's wearing her brother's Northwestern sweatshirt, and her braids trail down her back. *What is she doing here?* I wonder. She's school-friendly with Naomi (who writes advice for *The Argus*) and Lauren, but I thought she hated Caroline. I assume most people hate Caroline. We make eye contact just long enough for me to be sure she's wondering the same of me.

"You made it!" says AJ. She looks genuinely happy to see us—especially Mitch, whom she stands up to hug. A little comet of excitement shoots through me on his behalf.

"How's it going," he says, masterfully concealing his own happiness.

"We're just getting started," says Caroline, glancing somewhat self-consciously around the room. "I think more people are coming, but the snow . . ."

It is shocking to me that she cares whether we think her party is lively enough. It is, by default, already the biggest and wildest party that I've ever been to.

"Drinks are in the fridge," says AJ.

"Oh, yeah," says Caroline. "Help yourself."

Mitch points at me, asking if I want something, and I nod. He heads to the fridge, and I make my way to the floor-to-ceiling windows at the back. The house sits on a hill, and the yard slopes down on both sides like a very large bowl. Straight back is the lake, thoroughly frozen and obscured by snow. If it weren't for the dock, it would look like the property extended indefinitely. There aren't fences in the gated community, or sidewalks, or streetlamps; the houses are set far apart, separated by hills or trees or water: borders built and planted to make the exclusivity seem incidental. The lake isn't even real but man-made.

I can feel someone watching me, and I'm certain it's Hanna, so I pretend to be interested now in the vintage pinball machines to my right.

"Mary!" I hear AJ say. Her hand is cupped around her mouth, amplifying her lightly drunken holler. "Sit with us!"

All the seats on actual furniture are taken, so I move a few inches closer to the couches and obediently drop to the floor. I'm worrying AJ will feel like she has to talk to me because nobody else is—they've all continued hollering at each other over the music—but Mitch returns with our drinks just in time. My hero. I take my can of Coors Light and try to hold it like someone who's held a beer before. It looks not unlike a Diet Coke but tastes much, much worse. I notice Mitch watching me, smirking a little. "You get used to it," he says, then takes a swig of blood-orange San Pellegrino. I admire him so much for being able to not drink alcohol in this situation. I wish I felt similarly capable. But it would've been bad enough without Hanna, and yet she is here, ten feet away, and I don't know how we'll make it through the night without having to talk. Council and newspaper talk I can handle in the safety of school property, but something feels different here—like she might say anything. Certainly, the two empty beer cans in front of her make it more likely. I accidentally look right at her, and she notices immediately. We used to take so much pride in how in sync we were, our eyes trained to meet and agree we'd just experienced the same thing the same way, like our confirmation teacher's references to the always-pregnant junkie sister he'd clearly invented as a cautionary tale. I laugh a little to myself, thinking about "Jade" now.

"What?" says Mitch.

"Nothing," I say, and take another sip of beer.

It goes okay at first, all things considered. Mitch is by my side, and I mostly just talk to him, and the only real challenge is hearing each other the first time we say anything. We keep needing to lean into each other's necks, and the more I drink, the more romantic it feels, and the more I begin to wonder—again—if I made a mistake. This still feels like what I want, or what I'm supposed to want, and the distinction between these two things is even blurrier than usual. At one point I even prop my arm around Mitch's shoulders so I can say something directly in his ear, and he rests his hand on my back to support me. He is such a nice, *nice* guy, and not the way people usually mean when they say that.

The music gets louder, and more people show up. I am constantly aware of Hanna's position in the room, until I notice she's not there anymore. Around the same time I realize how badly I need to pee.

"Is there a bathroom?" I yell to Caroline. A dumb question.

"What?" she yells.

"Bathroom!"

She nods, comprehending at last. "Down the hall!" she shouts. I follow her thumb, but the hall is so long and seems to stretch the more I look at it. The two-thirds of a can of beer I've drunk is hot in my stomach. I know, instinctively, that Hanna is down that hall. I don't want to talk to her. I go after her anyway.

At the end of the ten-mile hallway is an open door to a dark home gym and two closed doors. Light seeps out from under one—presumably the bathroom—so I open the other just to see what happens. No secret couple leaping up, caught in the act. It's a guest bedroom, from the looks of it: sterile and small, furnished mostly in IKEA. I wonder if I could move in, how long it would take for anyone to notice.

Behind me I hear the bathroom door open. I hope I'm wrong. I look over my shoulder to check, and Hanna stands there, looking at me and then past me, into the bedroom.

"What are you doing?" she asks.

I want so badly for some chilly retort to come to me, but all I can think of is *None of your beeswax,* and it would be less embarrassing to shit my pants on the spot.

"Snooping, I guess," I say finally.

Hanna untenses, just barely. "Wait'll you see the bathroom," she says.

What happens next is the beer's fault. I know this as it's happening, and I let it happen anyway.

"Why aren't we friends like we used to be?" I say.

Hanna blinks at me. "What?"

"I mean, I guess I know the answer to that. You basically ditched me." My voice sounds like someone else's voice, someone powerful and mean.

"That's not what happened," says Hanna. She glances down the hall, which makes me do the same, but no one is coming to save us.

"What should I call it, then?" I say. "You stopped talking to me about anything real, and I've never known why."

"Are you serious?" she says. She's looking at me like she's concerned I might be crazy, which only makes me feel crazier. "We stopped talking to *each other*."

My face burns. "If you mean I eventually stopped trying after it became clear you didn't want to be friends anymore, then sure, that's true."

Hanna starts shaking her head in protest before I finish. "That's not what I mean at all. We both backed off at the same time, and you know exactly why."

I fling my hands around between us and shriek, "No, I don't! Clearly!"

Hanna blinks at me again. She seems genuinely confused. "Really?" she says, gentler than I expect. "At retreat? The bus?"

I have no idea what she's talking about. I think back on it: the bunks, the piles of letters on Hanna's bed and the single envelope on mine, the candles, the crying. I don't see anything there that clinched it. It was a bad weekend, but I never considered it the end of our friendship. Why would it have been? I shrug helplessly. I don't like the way Hanna looks at me now.

"Madison?" she prods.

Madison Nygaard: our confirmation class's scariest, holiest member. Voice of an angel. Huge gray eyes and hair so white it matched her acolyte robes. "What about her?"

Hanna stares, and I'm about to lose it when she looks down the hall and, finding it still empty, gestures for me to follow her back into the bathroom.

"What if someone has to pee?" I say when she closes the door behind me.

"There are four other bathrooms in this house," she says.

"I get it—you've been here before," I say, sounding so ridiculously bratty that we both laugh. I look around at the marble countertops, sliding-door shower, plush white towels, the scented-oil diffuser, the freshly cut tulips. "This *is* a nice bathroom."

"I told you. I've been here *several* times," she adds with a smirk.

I miss her. Or maybe it's the beer. My emotions feel smoothed and simplified: here is my former favorite person on Earth. Why isn't she still?

I take a deep breath and fold my arms across my chest to calm my nerves. "Tell me, then. What happened?"

Hanna, too, takes a grounding breath. "On the bus to the retreat, we were talking about our house."

My arms tingle in immediate recognition. *Our house.* I know exactly what she means: not her parents' house, or mine, but mine and hers. I don't remember talking about it on the bus, but I remember it so clearly, so quickly, though I haven't thought about it in so long: the garden on the hill, the sleepover room, the three-season porch. The guest homes way, way in the back, where our husbands would live, so that we, Hanna and I, could keep our house to ourselves.

"We were holding hands," Hanna continues. "Madison popped over the seat and saw us and told us we were weird."

My heart thuds in my throat. I can't tell if I remember it, exactly, or if I'm just picturing what Hanna has told me, but either way, it's there in my brain, and I know it's true. I can hear just how Madison would have said the word "weird," and I know what she would have meant. And I'm furious.

"So that was it?" I say. "You stopped talking to me because some bitch from private school implied we were . . . ?" I can't finish it. I'm suddenly worried that isn't what Hanna thought at all.

She looks at her feet, and when she looks back up, there are tears in her eyes. "It's not like I feel good about any of this," she says. "But we were kids."

"We were best friends," I say.

"You pulled your hand away first," she says softly.

I still don't remember that part, but I don't argue. It feels true. It is what Hanna remembers as true.

"Is that why you cried?" I ask. "That last night?" The connection only comes to me as I'm saying it.

Hanna cocks her head. "Let's not give Madison *that* much credit," she says. Which, I notice, is not a no.

"But it wasn't just that, was it?" I say. Other memories come to me now—how Hanna always wanted to run around outside and I just wanted her to watch me play video games. The time she told me I had to stop quoting *Monty Python* so much. The time we planned a two-night sleepover and called it short at ten the first morning because we had run out of things to say.

"We grew apart," Hanna says. "It started before the retreat."

There is something we're not saying, and I'm not sure I can be the one to do it. Did we pull apart because we didn't want people to see what Madison saw, or did we pull apart because she was right? Something about the way Hanna sounded when she said I withdrew my hand from hers makes me wonder. But maybe it doesn't matter. We used to love each other, but it's been so long. Now we only remember having loved each other when we were kids.

"Are you okay?" Hanna asks.

"Yeah," I say, though I'm not really sure. "Could I . . . could we maybe hug?"

Hanna smiles and puts her arms around my shoulders. We don't fit together like we used to, but we both do our best.

I try to remember what this used to feel like and whether it meant something more, but I can't. All I know is that it's different now. And all I can think about is what it would feel like if Elyse held me like this. I have this feeling my arms would know just where to go.

I release Hanna, and she lets go, too. "We should probably—"

"I still have to pee," I say.

"Okay, great," says Hanna. "Uh, you know what I mean."

I do. We exchange dumb little waves, and as she opens the door to leave, I stop her.

"Hanna," I say. She turns, questioning. "These are the best ones yet," I say, pointing to the phantom glasses on my own face.

She touches an arm of her chunky forest-green frames and smiles. "Thank you," she says. "I think so, too."

When she closes the door behind her, shutting me in, I feel so light on my feet I could lift off my toes, right into the air. I try it just in case: no. Oh, well.

I emerge from the bathroom and walk down the nearly endless hallway to a different sort of party from the one I left, however long ago that was. The lights are dimmed, and behind the couch there is now a makeshift dance floor. Two girls from the dance team perform an R-rated segment of their pep rally choreography while the boys watch over the lips of their beer cans. Hanna is back on the floor, talking to Naomi, and even though I wait a few seconds, she doesn't notice me looking. We are no longer so desperate to ignore each other that our eyes can't help but meet.

I scan the room for pink hair and find Mitch on the couch talking to Caroline. On Caroline's other side is AJ—not a coincidence, I'm sure—talking to Keely with big, dramatic expressions. I can almost feel her wanting Mitch to eavesdrop, and him trying just as hard to find a chance to interject.

I go to the fridge, pick out a sparkling nonalcoholic something or other, and settle into an open armchair close enough to AJ and Keely that we can all pretend I'm part of their conversation, even though, after they pause to acknowledge my presence, I'm not. Normally, this type of arrangement would stress me out, but right now I am grateful to have the alone time in this loud, fancy basement to drink my fruit juice and think.

The next thing I know, I'm opening my eyes to Mitch's hand on my knee. I look around and see that Caroline is also asleep, Keely and Tyler have their coats on, and AJ is picking up empty beer cans and dropping them in a garbage bag. The party has thinned, and the music is low.

"Time to go," says Mitch.

"Midnight?" I ask. I'm afraid to check my phone, but when he grins sheepishly I have no choice. It's 1:12 a.m., putting me an hour and twelve minutes past curfew. I find I'm too tired to care. I get up, smooth my hair, and watch AJ say goodbye to Mitch. She and I wave, and I look for Hanna, but she seems to have already left. Mitch and I head upstairs. He slips into his boots and coat so quietly, so efficiently: a practiced leaver of parties. I, on the other hand, leave my shoes untied and carry my coat in my arms into the freezing night.

The snow has stopped, and the clouds have cleared, and the ground glows blue-white. We sit in Mitch's car for a few minutes until it's warm enough to melt the windshield clear.

"Have fun?" he says.

"I don't know if that's the word I'd use," I say.

He laughs.

"Did you?"

"It was all right, yeah," he says.

"Talk to AJ?"

He smiles. "Just a little."

"Well, give it time," I say. "But I think she's into you."

"You talked to Hanna," he says, changing the subject. I look over, surprised. He must have noticed when we were both gone. I'd told him how we used to be best friends, until she ditched me. I have to revise that story now.

"I did," I reply. I plan to tell him more, but I lean my head against the window and fall immediately asleep, and suddenly I'm home, and Mitch is waking me up for the second time tonight. I reach across the console and hug him tighter than I ever could before.

"Thank you for everything," I say.

"Go to bed," he says, and I do.

My parents aren't up waiting. Even Peter's room is quiet and dark. *I could do anything*, I think as I get into bed. The whole house is mine.

———

I'm grateful to have the early shift at La Baguette, even though it means about five hours of sleep. Without it, I know, I'd be glued to my bed and my phone, thinking and googling and sending needy texts to Cara and maybe even Mitch. The implication of my discussion with Hanna hits me fully when I'm in the bathroom, brushing my teeth, and I have to sit down on the toilet. It is the first time I have ever brushed my teeth for a full three minutes in my life.

Last night's snow has been cleared from the roads, and white sparkling mountains line every street. It's sunny and warm enough to remember the notion of spring, which is a dangerous thing to think about when it's only thirty-two degrees and we're not yet halfway through January. Everything seems extra bright to me, which I know is a hangover symptom, though I'm not sure I can claim a hangover after drinking less than one beer. I catch myself making a mental note to google "hangover rules CDC NIH WebMD" later and groan. Sometimes I am so thoroughly myself it makes me sick.

I'm hyped up and nervous the whole drive, and for once I address it head-on. I am going to see Elyse today. I want to see her and talk to her. I like her. I think I might like her the way Madison accused Hanna and me of liking each other. I still can't remember the exchange on the bus, but I know Hanna was telling the truth. Why make something like that up? But also: Why forget it?

Some of these questions can wait for Kelly the next time I see her. I'm excited for that, too. Here she probably thinks I had a totally uneventful, unrevelatory winter break, when in fact I possibly became a lesbian. I pull into the parking lot, laughing to myself like a creep. I feel floaty and a little crazy, vaguely concerned with the way I'm reacting but unable to stop what's already in motion.

I walk into the restaurant to find Justin on a step stool, placing labels for today's soup options in the empty slots on the wall-mounted menu. "Good morning!" I chirp.

He gives me a strange look over his shoulder. "Morning," he mutters. He hates me, and that's fine. I don't like him, either.

In the back I pull my apron over my head and find my name tag in the bucket, seeing Elyse's there, too. My chest flutters just seeing her name, which feels like a bit much. *Calm down,* I tell myself. *Not so long ago you felt the same way about Mitch, and look how that turned out.*

But Mitch is my friend now. And maybe it wasn't exactly the same. How can I tell? I'm dawdling, taking ages to put on my visor and name tag, when Elyse bursts through the swinging doors. And I know: no, it isn't exactly the same. With Mitch there was always this underlying element of fear. I wanted something to happen, but mostly so that I could say it happened. I wanted it over and done with; love accomplished and aced like a final exam. Here, with Elyse, there is no fear. Only want. My cheeks flush beet pink.

"Hey!" she exclaims. She moves toward me for a hug, and this time I let myself feel all the things I didn't notice—or ignored—when she hugged me before. Right now I don't even care if she feels any of them, too. It is so thrilling just to know myself. But there is an unmistakable beat after we separate, smile at each other, and avert our eyes. Unmistakable—right? I try to imagine describing the moment to Cara and cringe at how silly it sounds: "we hugged . . . we paused."

"I guess we should clock in," says Elyse, and I let her lead us back through the doors. I glance at the hair on the nape of her neck, wanting to touch it. Until last night I didn't think of girls this way, but it's like a switch has been flipped or a wall has come down, and suddenly they have access to the part of me I thought was only available to boys. And, even then, only barely.

When La Baguette opens for the day and customers start coming in, I assess each woman with new eyes, trying to work out whether or not I'd kiss her if I could. *How many should I want to kiss?* I wonder. A customer asks me a question about soup, and I have to ask her to repeat it because I'm too busy scrutinizing my feelings about her face. It's sick.

"Is it made with beef broth or chicken broth?" she says slowly. She thinks I am stupid. *Fine*, I think, *we won't kiss.*

"Beef," I say. I do not know this. I just pick one.

"Uh, it's chicken," Elyse interjects. She gives me a quick *What's wrong with you?* look, and I'm embarrassed.

"Oh, right, sorry about that," I tell the customer. She smiles tightly at Elyse and orders the Asian chicken salad, no soup. I hand her a buzzer, and she takes it and walks off.

"I think I'm hungover," I mutter.

"How much did you drink last night?" she says.

"One beer," I say. "Almost." I smile as Elyse throws her head back in laughter. I decide she is the only person allowed to tease me.

I wait all shift for a break long enough to tell her about the Hanna revelation, but it never comes. And maybe I don't work that hard for a chance, either. The more I think about it, the less sure I am of what happened, or how to describe it to someone else, how what was said unlocked something in my brain or put a whole new concept there. Elyse will say she already suspected me, and then I will feel naive. Or she will think I'm telling her I like girls because I know she likes girls and I want the two of us girls to like each other. Which I do. I think. But I don't want *her* to think that I think the only thing keeping her from falling madly in love with me is my (former) heterosexuality.

It might help if I were an entirely different person: one who knows how to stop thinking and *Just do it* (Nike™). But there is only so much I can be expected to change in one twenty-four-hour period. This is what I tell myself as I drive home, having said nothing important at all to Elyse, feeling a little less light than before.

———

The night before we go back to school, Peter knocks on my bedroom door. I'm lying in bed, on my phone, listening to a band Elyse mentioned liking. I love them, of course.

"Come in," I say, expecting my mom and surprised to see Peter. I can't remember the last time he came into my room. He looks around at my desk and bookshelf and walls like it's unfamiliar to him, too. He stands there, then closes the door behind him, then hovers, staring at the floor and rubbing the back of his head. I remember when he used to buzz his hair in elementary school, and I'd run my hand over the same spot when it grew out just enough to move. He'd only let me touch him for a few seconds before yanking his head away.

"What are you doing?" he says now.

I hold up my phone. "Nothing."

He nods, glances again at the posters hung on my wall. Lots of boy bands, I realize now. Most of them I taped up in middle school, using blue painter's tape because my mom said anything else would damage the walls. Once a month or so the same three corners on the same three posters lift and curl away from the wall, and I have to go around smoothing them back down. For what? I get up from my bed and take them down one by one, rolling them up and tossing them on the floor.

Peter watches, bemused. "Were they just canceled or something?"

I laugh. "No," I say. "I just need a change." I sit back down on the bed and wait. It's clear he came in for a reason. Maybe there's a girl. Or a boy. I've been waiting my whole life for him to ask me for advice about a girl. (Or a boy.)

"There's something I need to tell you and it's probably not a big deal but if it is I'm sorry," he says, all in one breath. He is trying so hard to seem chill in all the same ways I try to seem chill: pointless shrugging, weird head tilts, avoiding eye contact. I must learn from this.

"How about you tell me, and I'll decide if it's a big deal or not?" I say slowly. I'm racking my brain for things he might have done to ruin my life lately, but I'm coming up short. It's pretty much all been on me.

He takes a deep breath and sits on the floor. He starts picking at the cream carpet, and I watch him discover the place where I spilled nail polish topcoat and, in a state of panic, cut off the tips of the fibers to try to mask it from our mom, leaving a small crispy divot.

"Last semester, in, like, the first or second week of school, you got me in trouble with Mom," he says.

I don't remember this, and I tell him so. That said, it sounds like me.

"It doesn't matter," he says, sounding frustrated. "I hadn't started studying, and you wanted the TV or something— that's not the point."

I remember now. I'd been absolutely desperate to watch *The Masked Singer*. Humiliating. I wait as he gathers the courage to continue. I feel faintly like throwing up.

"While you watched your show, I came upstairs, in here, and found your planner on your desk," he says. He gets quieter and quieter with every sentence. Soon I will have to read his lips.

"You just . . . came into my room," I repeat.

"Yeah," he says. "And I found your planner, and I saw that you hadn't even done all *your* homework after getting me in trouble for not doing mine."

A feeling like a hot bucket of water followed immediately by a cold one drops over my head, falling all the way to my toes. It was him.

"You crossed out my history homework," I say.

Peter looks at me, assessing whether or not he needs to get up now and run. He nods slowly.

I'm cold with fury, so I close my eyes and breathe. This whole semester—everything about my self-deterioration project, my unprecedentedly average GPA—it all started with a lie. I didn't make a mistake. I was sabotaged.

"Obviously, I didn't think it would make much difference," says Peter. "It was one assignment. You'd still get an A." He pauses, and I open my eyes to find him looking like he's going to cry. "I even forgot about it. But then we got our report cards. And then you said the thing about not doing homework anymore."

My mind reels, searching for the memory of finding my planner, seeing my homework crossed out, and going to bed, assured I'd done everything that had been asked of me. I must have intended to finish that night, though I always did my homework before dinner if I wasn't working at La Baguette. But I don't remember seeing the planner until the next day, when it was too late. I am beginning to seriously worry about early-early-onset dementia.

"I'm sorry," Peter says. Pleads, really. "I didn't mean to ruin your whole GPA."

"You didn't," I say quickly, surprising us both. The reflexive rage has passed, and now I just feel tired. "Everything after that assignment was my choice not to do."

"But why?"

I shrug. "It didn't seem to matter anymore."

Peter nods. "Most of it doesn't, I don't think."

"I really thought it did," I say. I trace my finger over one of the sunflowers on my quilt, careful to complete the full outline exactly before moving on to the next. "The more I talk about it, the dumber I feel."

"Which part—doing homework or not doing it?" he says.

"Both," I say.

"I don't think it's dumb to realize you don't have to do everything everyone tells you to do," says Peter. "I also don't think it's dumb to try."

I lay my hand flat on the quilt and study my brother for a second. He's gotten taller, I'm sure, even in the last ten minutes, sitting here on my floor. He tilts his head, second-guessing himself, and I know the quote that's coming before he says it, so I say it with him: "Do. Or do not. There is no try." Yoda.

He smirks, and I roll my eyes.

"We're hopeless," I say.

"Speak for yourself," says Peter. He shoots up from the floor but pauses at the door. "Are you gonna tell Mom and Dad?"

"No way," I scoff.

"As *if*!" says Peter, with a Cher-from-*Clueless* flick of the wrist.

"Okay, goodbye, you can leave now," I say, and he does, laughing as he pulls the door closed behind him.

Maybe I should feel angry or overwhelmed, but I don't. I feel instead the soft, firm weight of acceptance on my chest, the same feeling I get after I've stopped sobbing only because I've run out of energy to cry. Whatever's left in me is here to stay, so I might as well get on with it. In the span of a week I've learned that I was wrong about two fairly major moments in my own chronology, but I am still here. Nothing about the rest of my life is set in stone, and it feels good.

———

The first day back after winter break is, I think, superior to the first day back after summer vacation. This actually is an unpopular opinion. Everyone pretends to want an endless summer and to hate school, but by mid-August most of us are restless and desperate to show how much we've grown and improved since the year before. People walk into school in the fall believing in miracles, or at least in chaos.

But I like coming back to school after Christmas because it's predictable. You have your teachers figured out, and the coordinates of your locker are ingrained in muscle memory. It's January, and therefore freezing, which means the school is warm when you walk in, and the sun isn't up when the day begins. I realize this all sounds depressing, but it helps me to think of myself as a little blind bat, and of the school as my cave. Everyone's wan and lethargic, and there's solidarity in that. Fall semester is about the individual; spring semester is about the community. I explain all this to Peter on the drive to school, and when I've finished, he tells me to get a life. I tell him that's the goal.

I'd intended my first stop to be Cara, but as soon as I'm inside I find myself walking toward the student council room, where I know I'll find Ingrid. Every morning she gets to school forty-five minutes early, with coffee in hand, and sits at the head of the council table with a tented piece of paper on which she's written "TOWN HALL" in Sharpie, the idea being that student-citizens can use this time to speak with their elected leader directly. As far as I know, nobody has ever taken her up on it. Indeed, when I open the door, Ingrid is alone, with her coffee, reading a book. At the sound of the door her eyes shoot up, and she slams the book closed like I caught her with porn. Then she realizes it's me.

"Oh," she says. "Hey."

"Can I sit?"

She nods, gesturing to the seat farthest from her. I take it, and she sits up straighter, a look of determined diplomacy straining her jaw.

"Do you like all this?" I ask, gesturing around the fluorescent, ugly half room.

"What do you mean?" she says, but it seems she knows exactly what I mean, because she answers herself. "Council? Yeah, I love it."

"Are you sure you love it, or do you just think you're supposed to?"

She raises an eyebrow. "You're projecting."

"Yeah," I say. "No shit."

Ingrid sits back and crosses her arms, letting her pile of painted metal bracelets slide and clang into each other noisily. She has worn them every day that I've known her, regardless of accompanying outfit or au courant high school style. They are the loudest, most incongruous thing about her.

"I do love it," she says. "I like to be in charge, and I love having goals."

"But nothing ever changes," I say, somewhat apologetically. Suddenly I worry she hasn't noticed.

She nods. "Not much," she agrees.

"So what's the point?"

Ingrid shrugs. "Not everything needs a point."

We both pause, stunned by her profundity. *Is that what it is?*

"Is that true?" I ask.

"I don't know," she admits. "I need more coffee. You're stressing me out."

I laugh. I realize I miss her. Not so much Missy. Philip, a little. "I know you haven't replaced me," I say.

"Yeah. So?" says Ingrid. But she's hopeful. I can tell.

"Do you think I could come back?" I realize as I say it that I really hope she'll say yes. Not for my parents, not for my teachers, not for college, but for me. These are my people. Even Missy, whom I hate.

She blinks, pausing for drama. "We'd need to vote. The three of us."

"Is that a rule?"

Ingrid smiles. "It is now."

In class I pay attention when I am interested and daydream when I am not. In Spanish we're beginning the future perfect indicative: things that will have happened at a certain point in the future. *In a year, I will have finished. . . . In five years, I will have graduated. . . . In ten years, I will have married.* I love the sound of the verb *haber*'s irregular conjugation. *Habré, habrás, habremos.* It is a confident verb. In four years, I decide, I will have become fluent in Spanish: *En cuatro años, habré dominado el español.* Again it comes to me easily. All I do is think of what I want to say in English and then translate it, piece by piece. I love not knowing a word and finding it in my dictionary. *I love Spanish,* I think to myself. I love language, period. This feels like useful information to know about myself, more applicable to choosing a college than all the numbers and scores I thought it'd come down to.

Señora Nelson seems to see the joy on my face and smiles at me several times from her desk while we work on some exercises in our workbooks. After class she motions for me to come over. "You're back," she says.

"I'm back," I agree, though really I don't think it's the same me but a new one.

All morning I feel like Ebenezer Scrooge on Christmas after being changed forever by the three Christmas ghosts. There is a newness to every classroom, even though they're the same ones I spent last semester in. I see now that I wasn't really *there* there, despite my body's presence. And I don't mean it didn't count because I didn't do the homework. I mean that I was waiting and watching the clock. I think I might have been depressed.

I'd been thinking that the central dilemma of my existence was that I'm here and don't know why, but maybe I had that backward: I may not know why, but I'm here.

―――

I haven't been this happy to see Cara in months. We're not huggers, but as I sit across from her at lunch, at the same table we've shared all year, I reach across it to clasp her shoulders. She returns the gesture by patting my forearms.

"I missed you," I say.

Pat, pat. "Me too. Where were you? I barely heard from you all break."

"Working," I say, releasing her to open my bagged lunch.

"I was bored senseless," says Cara.

"How was Audrey's cabin?"

"Mmm." Cara shrugs. "It was okay. Her family's *really* into puzzles."

This confession thrills me a little, but while I would've clung to it a month ago, I now let it dissipate. They will be BFFs again the moment Audrey arrives, and that's okay. Their friendship has no bearing on my friendship with Cara. I sit up straighter, inflated by my own moral fortitude.

"There's something I want to talk to you about," I say. I see Audrey strolling over with a lunch tray and briefly debate making something up—"I'm growing out my hair"?—or spitting it out quick before she arrives, but instead I sigh and wait for her to sit.

"Hi hi hi," she says. "You went to a party at Caroline's house with Mitch?!"

Once again I'm being tested. Audrey is clearly put out that I was invited to a Caroline & AJ joint production and she was not, even though she wasn't in town. I give myself just a second of smugness. Am I supposed to believe Ebenezer Scrooge never felt smug ever again? After a single haunted Christmas?

"Yeah. It was last-minute," I say. "Possibly a pity invite on their part."

"I'm sure that's not true," says Audrey, clearly believing it is.

"Anyway, it was mostly uneventful," I say. "I had eighty percent of one beer."

Cara laughs. "Wow, wild child over here."

"Were AJ and Jonah together?" says Audrey.

"I couldn't really tell." I won't tell her that Mitch likes AJ, and not only because it's somewhat wounding to my ego. He is more my friend than Audrey is.

"What were you gonna tell me, then?" says Cara.

Again I consider lying. But there's something freeing in the idea of telling two people instead of just one. *Spread it far and wide,* I think. Saves me the trouble. Still, my heart threatens to fly from its cavity. My body is more nervous than I am.

"You know that girl Elyse, from my job?"

Cara nods.

"I like her," I continue.

Cara blinks. "'Like.'"

"Like, *like* like. Yeah," I say. I look at Audrey, who chews at me thoughtfully.

"Does she know that?" says Cara.

"No. Well, I don't know. But I haven't told her."

"Is she gay?" says Audrey.

"Yeah," I say.

"Are you?" Audrey asks, matter-of-factly, eating another forkful of barely unfrozen green beans.

"I guess," I say. "I'm definitely something."

"It would explain a lot," says Cara.

"Yeah," I agree.

"Wow, okay," she says. She claps her hands together in a get-down-to-business sort of way. "What's your plan?"

"Like. In life?"

Cara sighs, pinches the bridge of her nose. "To seduce Elyse."

"Having a girlfriend who goes to a different school would be, like. Very cool," says Audrey. "A boyfriend who goes to another school sounds made-up. But with gay people you don't question it."

"We're really lucky that way," I say.

Cara's lips pucker as she holds back a cackle.

I notice I don't feel antsy over this conversation the way I did when it was Mitch I was meant to win over. I'm not much more confident in my ability to win over Elyse, but I am ready to try. All of this still feels like a shock to me, but now that I've told someone, and said the words out loud, it also feels a little more true.

———

The next day I take my brown-paper-bag lunch to Kelly's office so I can see her without missing Spanish or staying late. She smiles when I walk in and points excitedly to her candy bowl. "I restocked the good stuff!" I'm so happy to see her I could cry.

"How was your break?" I ask, taking a fun-size Twix and a Reese's Cup.

"Too short," she says. "How was yours?"

I want to know more about her holiday, and her life in general, but I know she'll redirect if I try to ask. It takes a lot of restraint to have a job that essentially forbids you to talk about yourself. On the other hand, you get to listen to gossip all day long. Maybe I would like to be a therapist one day. Next year I'll take psychology, and maybe I'll take it AP. Only because I've heard the teacher's good.

"My break was . . . sort of eventful," I say.

"Oh yeah?"

"Yeah. I think I came out."

Kelly's face is open but expressionless. I wonder how long it took her to learn to do that. "You think?" she says finally.

So then I explain it: the party at Caroline's house, the bathroom conversation with Hanna, the bus scene I don't remember that untangled something in me anyway. I tell her about seeing Elyse at work and how it felt like seeing her for the first time, like windshield wipers had cleared my eyes and now girls were people I could want to be more than just friends with. I tell her about Mitch and AJ and how it made me happy for him instead of jealous. AJ should *be* so lucky, I say. I tell Kelly about coming out to Cara and Audrey—because I guess that's what it was—and how simple, even how underwhelming, it was. I keep laughing, even though I'm not sure anything I'm saying is funny. It feels like I'm performing a monologue I've been unconsciously rehearsing all my life. *Is what I'm saying really true?*

I finish recounting my story, and we both sit with it for a moment. In my mind, Kelly is reevaluating how she sees me. *How does Mary who likes girls seem different from Mary who liked boys?* I fidget with my ponytail, annoyed by its limpness.

"I'm so happy for you," says Kelly. "You seem like you've grown a whole lot in a really short period of time."

Years or even months ago I would have heard that last part as a challenge: I did something better than average, and therefore it was my duty to keep it up. But I don't hear it like that now.

"Thank you," I say. "I hope it's all true."

Kelly cocks her head. "What do you mean?"

"I don't know," I admit. I try to explain the thing about feeling rehearsed. "It's like every time I go through some rite of passage or do one of the things you grow up looking forward to, it feels somehow fake. Like, I know I'm gonna feel that way about graduation, and going to college, and if I ever get married someday." I pause to imagine it: a faceless bride, I guess? Revised gender aside, I immediately lose interest. "I feel like I'm gonna die one day, thinking, 'I don't know . . . seems fake.'"

Kelly laughs, and it's like drugs to me. Something calming and a little heavy, the way Cara describes her weighted blanket. "I think that's normal," she says. "Especially for those occasions that are supposed to 'mean something.'" Here she makes strange little air quotes that make me laugh.

"I'm sorry," I say. "For some reason that made me picture being, like, ninety-seven years old and a doctor telling me, 'You're dying.'"

Kelly gives us a moment to collect ourselves. She glances at the clock that hangs over the door behind me, and I know we must be almost out of time.

"Does our conversation feel real to you?" she says.

"What—this one?" I ask. I look around her office, like I might catch an errant hologram that gives it all away. But the room remains neat, cramped, familiar, save for a new potted plant on top of the bookshelf. *Best of luck to you*, I think. This place is windowless, and I've already watched three predecessors wilt and die over the course of my time here.

"Snake plant," says Kelly. "Supposedly impossible to kill."

"You'll find a way," I say consolingly, and she laughs.

"What about the way you feel about Elyse?" she continues. "Not telling Cara or me about it, but just how you feel about her."

"Yeah," I say. "Definitely." I blush, and Kelly smiles.

———

I've been thinking a lot about dying—not that I want to but that I will. Usually when the realization comes to me, it's nighttime and I'm in bed and the prospect of my death feels crushing and impossible at once, so I try to distract myself by scrolling on my phone or falling asleep. Death shows up unannounced, and I try to avoid it until it goes away. Lately, though, I look for it on purpose. Peter and I watch a documentary about some of the ways different cultures bury their dead, and I become obsessed with Tibetan sky burial, a practice in which a dead person is left on the edge of a cliff, exposed to nature, so that vultures will come pick at the body, carrying pieces away to wherever they nest. Peter thinks this is disgusting—he says he wants to keep his skin until it dissolves on its own schedule—but I find it beautiful. My body in flight, feeding something, making itself useful after I'm done with it. What use are my bones to anyone in the ground?

I ask Peter which, then, is his death rite of choice, and he considers for a few minutes, really taking it seriously. "I would like my body to be launched into space, so I can scare aliens," he says finally. And I have to admit, this option is also a great one.

———

What's weird about coming out, I'm finding, is that it's this never-ending series of possible disclosures to people I wouldn't otherwise update about my love life. At the mall with Cara one night, trying on a shirt that looks just like all my other shirts, the woman working the fitting room notices my necklace, the outline of a heart on a short silver chain. "I love your necklace," she says. She is maybe twenty-five years old and wearing pristine eye makeup, so she frightens me. "My boyfriend never gets me jewelry."

This is weird on a number of levels. One is that now I feel sorry for her, like I should comfort this stranger while wearing a T-shirt she knows isn't mine. Two is that the necklace is from my parents: a fifteenth-birthday gift I never, ever wear—except, for some reason, today. Three is that I obviously don't have a boyfriend, and may not ever have one. Am I supposed to tell her this, now that she's confided in me, assuming we have this thing in common?

Instead, I shake my head and say *"Men"* like I know what I'm talking about, and luckily she laughs and leaves it there. I do not buy the shirt. I repeat the story to Cara when we've exited the store, and she says she gets why I'm annoyed, but I can tell she doesn't quite. Is it my job to close that gap in understanding? I don't think it is. I decide I don't need or want to tell anyone else anything until I feel I have something to share. If that something is a girlfriend, and that girlfriend is Elyse, then great.

In order to make that hypothetical a possibility, I will need to talk to Elyse. I get my chance on a Tuesday 4:00 p.m. to 10:00 p.m. shift when Jerry is working but Justin—heavens be praised—is not. The night starts off slow, and I worry that Jerry will send Elyse or me home, but instead he chooses Tracy, who is newest and working the bakery. I like Tracy, but I am relieved to see her go. She's cut two hours into her shift: sixteen dollars, I'm guessing, after tax. But you can't think about your time here like that. It's too depressing.

Tonight Elyse is wearing a lime-green polo that I know for a fact would make me look jaundiced or possibly already dead. I feel frumpy in my baby blue and hope she doesn't hold the uniform against me. Twice I sneak off to the bathroom to re-apply lip tint and mess with my ponytail, aiming for Kelley O'Hara's volume and shine.

I have decided I will ask her out. It's the quickest way to find out what's going to happen, right? I could tell her about Hanna and my ensuing epiphany, and try to read her facial expressions, and then wait, and flirt gently, to see if she ever asks me out. This is what the old me would have done. But I have changed. I got worse on purpose to see what was left of me. And now I think I know. I don't want to wait around for other people to take the lead, or tell me what to do. I am afraid of what she will say but not so afraid that I won't do it. The point is to try.

I wait until we close and the customers are gone. We take our register drawers and our half-empty complimentary fountain drinks to the booth we like near the window and sit down to count the money we made and won't keep.

"So," I start. My throat is dry, and I take a sip of Diet Pepsi. *Awful.* "I've been thinking all night about how to ask you on a date."

Elyse looks up, surprised. She smiles, and I smile, and I know that this was worth it, no matter what happens next.

Acknowledgments

Many thanks, as ever, go to my YA dream team: Marisa DiNovis, my editor; Allison Hunter, my agent; and Natalie Edwards, her assistant. You guys made this one feel easy and inevitable.

Thanks also to my family: my parents, who raised my brothers and me to be curious, generous, kind, and a little weird. Thank you for always believing in us. Joe and Dan, I couldn't be prouder to be your big sister.

Some friends who contributed, each in their own way: Chiara (because I know an idea's a good one when you're excited about it); Julie (for getting me the job at Panera back in high school—sorry I was bad at it); Pilot (for starting the Rolling Library—look it up!); my beloved D.E.B.S. (for being you).

And finally, as always: thank you, Lydia, for everything.